Paradise of Exiles

Paperback original

Paradise of Exiles

David Tipton

Shoestring Press

Thou paradise of exiles
Shelley, *Julian and Maddalo*

Typeset by The Midlands Book Typesetting Company, Loughborough (01509 210920)
Printed by Quorn Selective Repro, Loughborough (01509 213456)

Published by Shoestring Press
19 Devonshire Avenue, Beeston, Nottingham NG9 1BS.
Telephone: (0115) 925 1827

First published 1999
© Copyright: David Tipton, 1999
ISBN 1 899549 34 X

Shoestring Press gratefully acknowledges financial assistance from
East Midlands Arts.

To Micaela, Sara Jane and Patrick

Chapter One

Outside it was already dark, but gazing between the iron bars in the window of her first-floor flat, Cathy Morales could see the jacaranda trees silvery in the street-lamps and beyond, the faint reddish glow of downtown Lima. As she stared out she heard the maid, an Indian girl, doing the washing-up in the kitchen. It had been one hell of a day. Non-stop rush since seven o'clock that morning. Getting the kids off to school, driving to the Catholic University where she taught English, back for lunch, taking the children down to the beach for a swim, home to prepare dinner in case her husband, Alberto, turned up, showers for the kids, then bedtime. Now at eight o'clock she had time to herself, to relax and work on some translations for the next issue of *Ayllu*, the magazine she edited.

'Maria!' she called to the maid. 'Bring me a glass and that bottle of *pisco, por favór.*'

'*Si, señora,*' Maria answered and a few minutes later, still wearing her white apron, appeared with *pisco*, ice and a glass.

'That's all then,' Cathy said. 'Don't forget to wake me if I sleep late tomorrow.'

'No, *señora, gracias.*'

Cathy lit a cigarette from the pack of Lucky Strike Alberto had brought home from his last trip to the north, poured herself a generous measure of the colourless liquor, added some ice, then sipped it appreciatively.

She hadn't seen Alberto now for two days and she'd no idea where he was. With his hippy friends, she supposed, listening to rock music, smoking dope and talking in endless circles. She didn't really care what he was doing, but at the same time resented his irresponsibility. It was as if he'd forgotten he had a wife and three kids to support. He would

1

give her money after one of his trips when he had successfully smuggled marijuana into the country, but she could never rely upon that. He received a salary as manager of his parents' chicken-farm in the hills, but most of that went on the rent. Moreover his parents had been threatening to give his job to someone else if he continued to leave the running of the hatchery almost entirely to the Japanese overseer.

She went into her small study, catching a glimpse of herself in the mirror near the bookcase. Her face looked drawn and tense. Only her blue eyes seemed to have stayed clear, untroubled. Ever since the birth of her third child four years before she'd steadily lost weight and no matter how much she ate or drank she couldn't put it back on. She burned up the fat with a restless, almost neurotic energy. She was too thin, Alberto would say, with no flesh where it mattered. This infuriated her. He left her to run the home on her own, then had the nerve, the insensitivity to complain.

She glanced through the rough drafts of her translations, but although they had been on her mind all day she no longer had the will to work at them. Sitting at her desk she wondered when it was that things had first begun to go wrong. Six months ago they'd been living in a Spanish-type ranch near the chicken-farm. A beautiful and spacious place with a swimming-pool in the garden, its white walls bright with bougainvillaea, set against the crenellated ochre foothills. Below it ran a tiny stream that flowed through a valley of vivid-green vegetation. There she used to take the kids for picnics, parking her battered VW under the eucalyptus trees lining the dust track that led up into the mountains.

She'd loved it at the ranch – the clear blue skies throughout the year, the weekly drives into the city to do some shopping or visit the cinema, the tranquility. During the winter they held weekend parties when their friends came to enjoy the warm sun while the coast was veiled in mist. She wasn't teaching then and had much more time for the magazine. But Alberto's parents were losing money. They'd had to sell the ranch. Now Alberto had to drive the twenty kilometres to the chicken-farm each day and he was becoming progressively more careless about his job, using it simply as an excuse to travel.

The hippy subculture was beginning to infiltrate the Lima middle-class and there was Alberto, a thirty-year old businessman, at the centre of a shiftless collection of writers, expatriates and rich unemployed society kids revelling in the flux of wishy-washy ideas, or so they seemed to Cath, that stemmed from a belief in the mind-expanding revelations of drugs and in doing whatever one wanted without moral obligations or scruples. It would have been laughable had it not been so alarming.

The trouble was Alberto had never really wanted to work for his parents or be a businessman in the first place. At first she had sympathised with him, but now it was necessary unless he was prepared to use his fluency in languages as a translator. But Alberto had always had money and couldn't take work seriously. Nothing would change him, not even his parents' dwindling fortune. He'd always been able to get handouts from them and seemed content enough to rely on that, even though financial dependence meant he was tied to them and this seemed to her a sign of his immaturity. She had even been thinking of going back to the States and getting a job there. It was one of the reasons she did the translations. Publication would stand her in good stead were she to leave.

Coming from a working-class New England background, her family Irish by descent, she'd had a fairly tough childhood, working her way through university with perseverance and determination. Even after eight years of marriage some of that old insecurity still infected her. She worried about things Alberto regarded with an irritating nonchalance. Temperamentally they were quite different, divided by a wide enough gulf of attitude and experience. She'd met him while studying Peruvian literature on a scholarship at San Marcos University and he'd seemed unlike any of the men she'd known before. Tall and broadshouldered, with a degree in agriculture from a college in California, he spoke English with a West Coast accent and had just been demobbed after three years with the American Marines. Easy-going, generous, with an ability to talk well about almost anything – an accomplishment acquired through extensive travel with his father who had been in the Peruvian diplomatic service – he had certainly attracted her.

When she'd found herself pregnant she was slightly hysterical, but Alberto accepted it in his good-humoured way.

'Let's get married,' he'd said and after a week or two of vacillation she had agreed. It would interrupt her career, but that seemed a small sacrifice to make. Secretly she believed she'd done well for herself though she smiled now at the irony of that. There had in fact been obstacles from the start. Alberto's parents regarded Cathy as a bit of blue-stocking, a self-seeking *gringa*, far too forthright and assertive, but it was precisely her air of independence and academic accomplishments that fascinated Alberto. His parents wanted him to marry a more decorative, a more domesticated girl. They doubted whether Cathy would make him a good wife at all. Fortunately she was a Catholic and in the end this smoothed away their opposition.

At first things had gone well. She had three children in five years, proved herself to be a conscientious mother and ran her household with an efficiency his parents could scarcely complain about. Alberto, once a source of anxiety to them, appeared to have settled down into the family business and taken his responsibilities seriously. Marriage had been good for him, they decided.

Cath was by now into her seventh *pisco* and too pleasantly mellow to work on the translations. She put them away, deciding to wait until Rick Preston returned to Lima in a few days time. She had worked with Rick before and trusted his judgements. Together they were going to edit the next issue of *Ayllu*. Now she would have an early night and try to catch up on some sleep.

Just after midnight she was woken up by a Rolling Stones record on the Stereo. She slipped out o bed and went into the lounge. Alberto had returned.

'Where have you been?'

'Honey, I'm sorry,' he said. 'I got invited along to this party where someone had LSD.'

'You mean you've been tripping for the last two days?'

'I dropped some acid, yes.'

'Jesus! I've been out of my mind with worry.'

'It was fantastic,' Alberto said. 'You must try some, Cathy, it's great stuff.'

Paradise of Exiles

She noticed that his eyes were heavy and bloodshot. He didn't give a damn about anything anymore, she thought, catching a whiff of stale marijuana and stale sweat. He'd put on weight over the last few months too. His paunch, flabby through too much beer and too many late-night snacks of rice and beans in all-night bars, drooped over his belt when he leaned forward.

'You look a mess,' she said.

'Come on, don't start moaning, I've not seen you for a couple of days.'

'And whose fault is that?'

'Mine, OK, but it's still a fact. Look, Cath, what's the problem? We've been all right for bread since I got back from Colombia.'

'You've just got to get a grip of yourself,' she said. 'Can't you see that our marriage is coming apart at the seams?'

'No, I can't frankly.'

'You haven't slept with me for weeks to start with.'

'Why do you think I spend so much time away? It's because you're always analysing things when I'm here, creating problems when there aren't any.'

'Alberto, you don't seem to realize which comes first – your drugs and music and unexplained absences or my so-called complaining. I don't care if you're sleeping with someone else, if you've got yourself a girlfriend, but I do care that I hardly ever see you and neither do the kids. Do you know you're likely to lose your job? Your mother has been phoning me up, asking where you are. It's embarrassing not knowing, having to make excuses for you and I can't take too much more of it, that's the truth. As a matter of fact I've been thinking of taking the kids and going back to New York.'

'If that's the way you feel, you can go, but you're certainly not taking the kids.'

'I wouldn't leave them here and that's for sure.'

'Cathy, I'm drained. Let's talk about all this tomorrow.'

'That's right, *mañana*. It's always the same. Evade the issue, skate over the problems.'

'I've got to be at the hatchery at seven in the morning.'

'All right, but we've got to talk about things. All this uncertainty is

5

driving me crazy. Incidentally, I got a letter from Rick Preston today. He and Jean are arriving on Saturday and I'd like you to be there with me to meet them.'

'That's great,' Alberto said. 'Of course, I'll be there.'

'They've got three kids themselves now. It won't be the same as it was before, you know. Parties, travelling all over...'

'I don't suppose Rick has changed, not for a minute.'

'He's got three young children to think about now. He's in the same position as you are.'

'Domesticity!' Alberto said. Cath gave him a quizzical look, but didn't reply. Nothing she could think of seemed adequate to express her feelings.

Tall and slim, Julio Scorza, crouched on the beach at Barranco skimming pebbles across the smooth surface of the water. To his left were the hunks of arid cliff and the jetty at Chorrillos with its brightly-painted fishing-boats. On the far side of the bay he could just discern the mauve outline of San Lorenzo Island and the port of Callao whose blurred buildings seemed to sprout from the sea. Behind him narrow cobbled steps led up past Barranco Baths through a suburb of balconied wooden-houses, their trellises a jigsaw of crimson, orange and magenta bougainvillaea and their patios shaded by mature bushy palms. It was the old artists-quarter where wealthy nineteenth-century writers and painters had lived. Julio had just been visiting a group of poets who still gathered for meetings at a house there. He had left abruptly in the late afternoon disgusted by the parochial nature of the poems that had been read, the old-fashioned rhetoric, the imitation and worn-out surrealism, the stock Marxist sentiments and the accompanying flattery that replaced any constructive form of criticism.

The sun was still warm. Julio watched the flat pebbles ricochet across the lagoon-calm surface of the water. Distracted by the cries of some children he turned towards the cliffs. At this point little streams that flowed underground from the foothills emerged and cascaded down the cliff-face, forming natural pools at the bottom. Sap-green trailers and vines clung to the rock.

Julio saw some Indian children standing under the waterfall, laughing and shouting while their father soaped them down. Brown-skinned and high cheekboned, the father was not that different from Julio in appearance, but Julio himself felt apart and alienated. The family was probably from the shanties whereas he, Julio, had been born into a middle-class family that owned land in the north. He had finished his education in the U.S.A. He read the poetry of Ezra Pound and William Carlos Williams. He spoke fluent English. Though not exactly wealthy he had never had to worry about money.

For four centuries the Indians had been exploited by the Spanish and Julio, though he felt sympathy for them because he was part-Indian himself, was by culture and heritage European, or Western at least. He had little sense of his identity as a Peruvian though he sought to define that identity in his poetry. He could only appreciate his country's legendary past as an outsider, like a tourist. It scarcely seemed to belong to him. If he went to Machu Pichu or Chan Chan he did so in the same spirit of curiosity as did Cathy Morales, or indeed any foreigner. But if he could assimilate the techniques of writers such as Pound and Williams he felt he might be able to create a genuinely-Peruvian poetry that would be both new and relevant.

The writers he had been visiting in Barranco, at the house they called the Tower of the Hallucinated, didn't have the same ambition at all. They invented charming names for their houses and for their books. They produced charming, but vaguely nostalgic verse that had no relevance to the present. They were locked in their ivory tower.

> *'I love a certain shadow, a certain light*
> *that gives a pale blue tint to the places of the dead.'*

Though he didn't admire them particularly those two lines which someone had quoted that afternoon stuck in his mind. As he had told them they mixed a little Lorca, a little Vallejo and a little Neruda with their social theories and called it poetry. And they had made a martyr of their friend, Javiér Heraud.

Heraud had studied in Cuba, not the States as Julio had done, and re-entered Peru via its jungle frontier to fight the government. He'd been shot as a guerrilla near the Madre de Dios River in 1963 and was now a symbol for a whole generation of poets. But Heraud had been a fool to destroy himself and his talent at the age of twenty-one. It was a stupid and futile tragedy.

After Heraud had been mentioned that afternoon, Julio referred his friends to the poetry of Pound and Williams, but they'd scoffed. Pound was a reactionary, a bloody fascist and Williams was a doctor feeding off a society that exploited the Third World, they said. How argue with such prejudice? How reason with such people? Heraud was their hero, not because he was a great poet – at twenty-one he had only just started, but because he'd fought as a guerrilla. It was immaterial whether that cause was right or wrong, a poet's job was to survive.

They admired revolutionary poets who wrote lines such as:

> '... To the wall with suffering,
> to the wall with the father of the lamb,
> to the wall with poetry itself
> if it fails to celebrate the revolution ...'

But poets had to be judged by their work, not by their sentiments and Marxism supported a host of mediocre versifiers. Writers in Peru felt guilty about Heraud because they themselves were only guerrillas in cafe discussions, but it was no excuse for deserting technique and hard work. Poets were in an ambiguous situation everywhere, but especially in Peru if their work failed to encourage social change or was obscure and difficult. It should be clean and transparent, written from inspiration according to the Romantic tradition.

Julio stood up and hurled a pebble far out into the sea. It wasn't enough to lean on the Puente Ricardo Palma, surveying the brackish waters of the Rio Rimac and meditating upon the Classics like some South American T.S. Eliot. It wasn't enough to suffer like Vallejo, dying in poverty in a foreign city. One had to try and get as wide a range of reality into one's work as possible – be a sort of literary monk with a passion for work that exceeded all else to produce something worthwhile. That was what he had tried to get across to those fools in their Tower of the Hallucinated. But they'd laughed at his anger and mocked his ideas.

On an impulse he stripped off to his underpants and dived into the sea. The cold and sharp tang of salt were exhilarating. He swam out through the line of surf, turned and gazed at the cliffs with their strips of emerald foliage. The Indian family was stretching out its washing on the shrubbery and the maze of houses in pastel shades decorating the rift was like a Cubist painting. Behind him the sun was setting in a red haze. The sea was cobalt, metallic and the white skyscrapers of the distant city were suffused in an amber glow. A window high up on some building caught the sun's reflection and momentarily dazzled him.

His anger evaporated like a hangover in the enveloping waves and he swam easily back to shore. He would walk into Miraflores, have a drink at the Haiti, go for a meal, then perhaps to the Zanzibar where they played folk and rock or the Golden Gate, an American bar, dark and glittery, with its jazz trio and freelance whores.

Alberto was sitting at a table outside the Haiti drinking a lager and idly watching the lights of the fountain that changed every few seconds from orange to blue, then to crème-de-menthe and rose. Some people were coming out of the Odeon and getting into cars. Small Indian boys rushed from one vehicle to another picking up the coins they'd earned by guarding them. A necessary service and good trade for the boys though they probably paid some of their earnings to the potential thieves.

Alberto put his lager down and lit a cigarette. However much Cathy complained he couldn't remain in her company for long these days. The urge to get out of the house was uncontrollable. It made him feel guilty but his relief was greater than his guilt. And if he wasn't away on some trip he made sure he was late returning home, or a little stoned, anything to avoid showing her physical affection. Recently sex with her had seemed like a lie. He was almost frightened of making love in case she mistook his intention and tried to control him through it.

A young Indian girl came over to his table and tried to sell him a bunch of violets which she'd probably nicked from the park.

'Shouldn't you be in bed at this time of night?' he said. 'Don't you have to go to school tomorrow?'

'I help my mother,' she said smiling. 'Sometimes I go to school, but in the afternoon.'

Alberto gave her ten *soles* and refused the violets. She insisted on his keeping them. He put them down on the table next to his drink. A woman passed clinging to the arm of her escort and laughing with a sensuous flirtatiousness. Alberto watched her hips swaying down the street. He could fancy almost any stranger though the idea of involvement turned him off too.

He ordered another beer, then caught sight of Julio Scorza approaching the cafe.

'*Hola, amigo,*' he shouted. 'How's things?' Julio sauntered over to the table and sat down, clapping Alberto's shoulders by way of greeting.

'I've just come from the Golden Gate,' he said. 'It's like a morgue in there. I was on my way to the Zanzibar. Do you fancy going?'

'Let's have a smoke first.'

'Grass?'

'Yeah, Colombian.'

'I wondered why I hadn't seen you around. You've been up to the north then?'

'As far as Buenaventura. That's a wild place.' Entering the port Alberto had been in the bows of a little cargo-ship, the lagoon calm and brackish, the land smell fragrant in a light breeze. A bottle-nosed dolphin had scratched its back against the rusting hull as they'd approached the shore, the ship edging its way through silted water to the docks. Black spidery shacks lined the white beach and the town above was a mass of corrugated-iron roofs.

'Did you score then?'

'The place is rotten with it,' Alberto said smiling. 'Let's go down to the *malecón* and have a joint or two and I'll tell you all about it.'

Alberto paid his bill and they walked down the street to his Volkswagen. He tipped the Indian boy who ran out from some shop doorway, opened the door for Julio. They drove down to the cliff at Miraflores. They smoked for a few minutes in silence. For the first time that day Alberto began to feel an expansive mood. Images of Buenaventura floated like film through his mind. The steep narrow streets, the shacks with wooden balconies painted blue and red, the

Paradise of Exiles

gawdy neon adverts that jutted across the streets. Exploring the place he'd felt like a contemporary buccaneer, but the bars were indolent and tranquil, full of *mulata* whores in tight cheap dresses.

'It was like a huge brothel,' Alberto said. Julio laughed. He too was enveloped in a cloud of benevolence, his anger of the afternoon completely gone.

'Strong stuff this.'

'The best,' Alberto said laughing softly. 'I had this old swordstick of my father's with me. A beautiful weapon, lethal.'

'A swordstick?'

'Just in case, but, man, the only time I was accosted was when a small black kid crawled across the street, his legs withered and useless. Made me feel guilty, tell you the truth, that boy just holding out a hand and moaning.'

'Oh there's going to be trouble one of these days,' Julio said. 'How long can people go on waiting for change, for some sort of equality?'

'I've seen beggars in Lima, but Buenaventura was full of them,' Alberto said. 'Beggars and whores. After I'd done the business I picked up this black chick. You know, man, sometimes I prefer whores. A pure financial transaction. No hang-ups, no sentimentality, straightforward, simple.'

'Nothing's simple. They're victims of the system and pressures you can't begin to imagine. As a wealthy foreigner you were exploiting her economically.'

'A whore's a whore anywhere and this one didn't seem unduly concerned. I paid her well and she gave me a good time. Christ, I saw girls in some bars no older than fourteen going with big German and Scandinavian seamen!'

'Barbarians,' Julio said. Alberto had lit their third joint and their thoughts were shooting off at a tangent, the sequence and logic of the conversation becoming muddled. The word 'barbarian' brought only an image of the girl to Alberto's mind. Bronze-skinned, languid, smiling lazily.

'She was like one of Gauguin's nudes,' he said. 'Earthy and sensual.'

'Don't romanticise debauchery,' Julio said. 'It's been done before and better. Read Baudelaire.'

11

Alberto chuckled. Walking through the garish streets after his night with the girl, he had been confronted by a woman waving the stump of her arm in his face, pleading for a dollar, mistaking him for a *Yanqui*. High on marijuana as he was now he had felt curious rather than appalled. The exotic was too much and sometimes dope was really necessary. That clammy morning he'd strolled to the top of the hill, content to be alone, his blue denim-jacket and hooped jeans singling him out as a tourist. Beneath him the palm-fringed beach was covered in detritus – old car-tyres, tin cans, rotting fish, little huts nestling on stilts in the mud. The street was lined with stalls selling mango, papaya and pineapple. Washing draped the bushes and young men were selling machetes. An incongruously sky-blue or pink Cadillac would occasionally bounce along the street, scattering the crowd. But when the ship sailed that evening, the stilted huts and puce-coloured water lapping the shore seemed beautiful. As they edged out of harbour he heard the stray sound of a guitar and the murmur of a woman's voice singing in the darkness.

Alberto checked his watch. Only twenty five minutes had elapsed since he'd parked the car.

'Let's go on to the Zanzibar,' he said, turning on the ignition, putting the VW in reverse and backing out. 'It'll be closed in an hour or so.'

'By the way,' Julio said as they were driving back. 'Is Cathy still bringing out the next issue of *Ayllu*?'

'I think so. She's totally immersed in translations anyway. I asked her if she wanted to come out this evening, but she refused.'

'I like her drive,' Julio said. 'And there's no magazine to touch *Ayllu* in Lima.'

'The next issue features a selection of your poems, doesn't it?'

'Yes, but that's not the reason I praise the magazine. I like its standpoint and the way Cathy introduces American poetry alongside Peruvian.'

They pulled up outside the Zanzibar. The club was part of an old colonial house with cedar-wood shutters and balconies shaded by palms and jacaranda trees. Inside were several wooden tables with trestle seats. There was a bar at one end and a small stage at the other.

It was a rock night and the DJ was playing records by the Rolling Stones. It was considered a chic and far-out place, the Zanzibar, by the middle-class students who frequented it and Alberto disposed of much of his marijuana there.

'You remember Rick Preston?' Alberto said when they were drinking a beer at one of the tables.

'I never met him.'

'Well, he's coming back to Lima at the end of the week,' Alberto said. 'And going to help Cathy edit *Ayllu*.'

'David León knew him quite well. Told me he had met him recently in London.'

'Whatever happened to León?'

'He's lecturing in England. I think he'll stay there. Little to bring him back here, not now. I don't know why Preston's coming back. He's in for a shock if the army takes over, and I think it will. It's not going to be such an easy-going place for *gringos*.'

'There'll never be a revolution,' Alberto said. 'Not here.'

'Don't be so sure, I've heard plenty of rumours. Besides, we need one, for God's sake.'

'It would end up the same – another bunch of crooks in power.'

'Believe it or not, there're quite a few Marxists in the army these days. Most of the young colonels were educated in the States, but have got their ideas from the guerrillas they were hunting not so long ago.'

'I thought the guerrillas had been wiped out since Ché's death.'

'Not all of them. Guevara was mistaken though. Revolution must start in the city, not with the Indians in the sierra, they're too passive, too bloody resigned. They've been repressed and exploited for centuries and haven't the heart to revolt. It's in the shanties that you'll find your support.'

'Did you know Javiér Heraud?'

'Yes, he was just a sensitive, middle-class boy educated at an English school,' Julio said. 'Then he went to Cuba to study film technique. So did León incidentally. Both were invited to switch to a course on guerrilla tactics and urged to return to Peru and set up communist cells

13

among the Indians. Doomed from the start, but Heraud was naive. Read his poetry – limpid verses about the beauty of Peru, brilliant but naive.'

'And León?'

'He turned down the offer and was thrown out of Cuba, so the story goes. That's why he's still detested by some of the so-called intellectuals here. They call him a coward. Ironically, of course, because they're all armchair Marxists. León had the good sense to see the futility of becoming a martyr to the cause in some godforsaken jungle. He's a poet, not a guerrilla. You are the sort, Morales, that should be doing the fighting.'

'I had enough of the army in the States. Anyway, I've got no political axe to grind. Rotten as it probably sounds, the status quo suits me.'

'Well, your family's well-off.'

'I'm not though, but if I were to become a revolutionary I'd be at war with my whole goddamn family. No, I believe in change through legislation.'

'It'll never come that way.'

'I don't know, but, man, enjoy the music, have another joint, marijuana's the revolution.'

'The trendy one,' Julio said. 'But it's a bit of good stuff, I must admit. I'm floating, high as a kite. But I shall have to go, I've got work to do tomorrow.'

'You've got a job?'

'I mean my poetry. My Peruvian Cantos or my Portrait of the Poet as a young Peruvian.'

'Have another beer?'

'No, really. You know the trouble with us,' Julio said. 'We're too pleasure-loving and we're too soft. There was a lot of sympathy with the guerrillas three years ago. Know what alienated a lot of the people?'

'What?'

'They tortured some police up in the mountains. Put red-hot stones in their armpits, or something. That was what the newspapers claimed anyway though it was probably all government propaganda.'

'It's all barbarism,' Alberto said. 'Go on home, Scorza, go and write your poems and I'll have another beer on my own.'

'See you then,' Julio said. 'Peace,' he added smiling.

Although it was gone midnight Alberto didn't feel like leaving. The beer and grass had put him into a mood of euphoria that not even Julio Scorza's analysis of the political situation had affected. Cathy would be in bed by now, if not asleep. There was no point in him having an early night. Several people greeted him at the bar, but he no longer felt like banal conversation with vague acquaintants he'd had dealings with.

Looking round he noticed Robert Redman, a journalist on the *Lima Herald*, with his American girlfriend, Sheila, sitting at one of the tables. Tall, with straw-blonde hair, Sheila, so Alberto had been informed, had once trained to be a nun. Looking at her now he found this hard to believe. She was dressed in a long skirt with some Indian motif embroidered upon it and a brown llama-wool poncho.

He watched them in conversation, Robert's black crinkly hair and neat Van Dyke beard, head bobbing in agreement with something Sheila said. Alberto had never particularly liked Robert. He was too tight with money, self-opinionated and prejudiced against Peru though half-Peruvian himself. His English father, a professional footballer, had come to Peru as a coach in the thirties and married a girl from Lima. Robert had been educated in England, only returning to Peru to help out his mother after his father had died of a heart-attack. There had been openings for people with bilingual ability then and he'd obtained his position on the English language paper. He wrote articles on offbeat places in Peru, interviewed foreign celebrities who visited and wrote film and book reviews. He seemed to know everyone in the expatriate community and sometimes held big parties. For this reason Alberto found him a useful contact.

Suddenly, as if sensing that he was being observed, Robert turned in Alberto's direction. He nodded towards him and raised his glass.

'Who were you waving at?' Sheila said.

'Alberto. Over there by the bar. He looks drunk again or more likely in a haze of hashish.'

'Let's go and talk to him.' Sheila was curious about all of Robert's friends, especially those with a literary bent. And Alberto, she knew, was also a source of dope. On the crest of her reaction against the

15

discipline imposed upon her in the convent Sheila was keen to try anything remotely illegal, or sinful. Before Robert could reply she began to push her way towards Alberto.

'Long time no see,' she said.

'I've been up to Colombia.'

'Have you heard that the Prestons are arriving on Saturday?' Robert said having followed Sheila to the bar. 'We'll have to organise a party to celebrate.'

'I know, Cath had a letter.'

'Is Rick taking over the magazine?'

'They're going to edit it together, or so Cathy says. You haven't met the Prestons, have you, Sheila?'

'I've heard a lot about them. Rick's one of Robert's heroes,' she said. 'And Jean seems to be some sort of mother-figure in Robert's eyes.'

'You'll like her, Alberto said.

'Robert regards her as some kind of saint.'

'That's nonsense,' Robert said.

'It's the way you go on about her.'

'She's simply a very tolerant and attractive woman,' Robert said. 'God knows how she puts up with Rick.'

'Rick's all right,' Alberto said.

'Now don't misunderstand me, I'm fond of Rick. When he was over here before he was probably my closest friend. It's just that he never seemed to fit the image I have of a responsible and loving husband.'

'Who does?'

'Where is Cathy, incidentally?' Sheila asked. 'I haven't seen her for quite a long time.'

'She was tired tonight, she stayed at home.'

'You Peruvians!' Sheila said. 'It's awful the way you treat your women. Leaving them at home to look after the kids and the house. It's archaic.'

'Cath never wants to go out. Join me for a beer?'

'We were just going,' Robert said.

'No, we weren't,' Sheila said.

'I was, I've got to be at the office tomorrow morning. The editor wants to see me. He's got some assignment, I told you.'

'But I wanted to talk to Alberto about his trip to the north,' Sheila said.

'Let's skip it,' Alberto said. 'I ought to be going myself soon.' He didn't feel like a flirtatious conversation with Sheila. In some ways she reminded him of Cathy when they'd first met. The same enthusiasm, the same ingenuous surface that concealed, he felt, a certain predatory quality. Besides, the effect of the marijuana was beginning to wear off. He had begun to feel a little paranoid, a bit touchy about criticism no matter how lighthearted or flippant.

'We'll probably see you at the airport,' Robert said. 'Perhaps we can arrange something for the weekend.'

Outside Robert and Sheila walked along Avenida Ricardo Palma towards their flat. There was a faint odour of salt on the breeze that blew in from the Pacific. It mingled with the smell of ground coffee as they passed the Tiendacita Blanca, a café by the fountain, and the tang of lemons from some patio.

'Did you notice Alberto's eyes?' Sheila said. 'They were all bloodshot and yellow.'

'He's a fool,' Robert said. 'He's been on drugs again. One of these days he's going to find himself in trouble. Too many people know about him already.'

'I don't think his marriage is in good shape either.'

'I feel sorry for Cath despite the fact that she kicked me off the magazine. She's having a tough time at the moment.'

'It's her own fault,' Sheila said. 'I wouldn't stand for such cavalier treatment. Besides, there're always two sides to that sort of situation. She's burning up with ambition and neurotic energy.'

'What about us getting married?' Robert said.

'Not here, I told you. Let's wait until we can go to the States. Give it time. I'm not exactly impressed by the marriages I've seen recently.'

'I'm crazy about you, you know that, don't you?'

'Marriage scares me,' Sheila said. 'It always seems to spoil things and I don't want our relationship to spoil.'

They passed the pyramid-shaped *huaco*, a restored Incaic burial mound, then strolled through the *bosque*, an olive grove full of twisted and gnarled trees that assumed grotesque shapes in the moonlight. Robert couldn't help feeling a certain complacency when he thought of Alberto and Cathy. They reached their flat in Conquistadores and inside he glanced round the newly-decorated living-room with a glow of pleasure. He touched the books on the shelves, re-arranged the folders on his desk, briefly examined the abstract paintings on the wall. Then he joined Sheila in the bedroom.

Chapter Two

The engines of the VC10 jet droned on monotonously. Rick Preston lit another cigarette and turned to look at Jean, his wife, dozing beside him, then he checked his two daughters who were stretched out on the seat behind them. With her blue eyes and reddish-gold hair, Sara who was nearly four resembled her mother while Emma, who was two, looked a little more like Rick himself except that she had hair the colour of burnished copper. David, the baby, lay sound asleep in his carry-cot at their feet.

Momentarily Rick wondered whether he had done the best thing bringing them back to Lima. He knew the dangers of returning to a place after an interval of eighteen months and in radically different circumstances. He would probably have turned the offer of a contract down had not Jean wanted to return. She appeared quite untroubled by doubts such as his though he couldn't be sure of this. He was rarely too sure of her feelings or reactions. He accepted their marriage as something that was permanent and durable, but often had the uneasy feeling that Jean had changed more than he had. She was more practical in many ways, perhaps more mature, more responsible. But the important thing was that they were still good friends.

The lights flashed on. They would be landing soon. Jean woke up and began to get the children ready. Seatbelts were fastened, their hand luggage packed as the plane banked over the sea, turned and came in to land. Through the window Rick could see the shape of mountains, then ahead of them the purple marker-lights on the runway. He stared out, saw the ground rushing beneath him, felt the bump of the wheels as they touched tarmac, and smiled at Jean.

Off the plane it was still dark. Because the airport staff were tired their cases were checked in cursory fashion and they were passed through documentation quickly. Then they were in the gleaming foyer with its black marble and shiny escalators, modern and somehow reassuring. Suddenly Rick caught sight of Alberto and Cathy. Just behind them were Robert Redman and a blonde-haired girl he supposed was Sheila. He waved and hastened over to them, Jean following with the children. They greeted each other, all talking at the same time, then Alberto grabbed the heaviest of the cases and started for the carpark.

'Come on,' he said. 'We'll get you to your new apartment.'

It was almost dawn, an etiolated grey light in the east, as they drove through the empty suburbs. Rick and Sara were in Alberto's car; Jean, Emma and David rode with Robert. As they sped along the coastal road, Cath talked continuously, but Rick still vaguely uneasy in the strange yet familiar city was only half-listening.

'I'm sure you've done the right thing coming back,' Cath was saying. 'You'll find lots of changes, and the cost of living's higher for sure, but it's still a good country . . . I've been working on some new translations, recent stuff by Julio Scorza, he's a great poet. As soon as you've got settled in I'd like to go over them with you . . . Sometime this weekend we can all go to the beach for a picnic perhaps, the weather's been quite warm and summery the last few days . . . Oh and Alberto's got lots of things to tell you, there's so much to talk about and catch up with . . .'

'I've been going up to the north,' Alberto said. 'Just got back from Buenaventura as a matter of fact.'

'On business?'

'Sort of – marijuana! There's loads of it and it sells like crazy down here now.'

'You mean you smuggle it in?'

'I wouldn't put it exactly like that,' Alberto said laughing. 'Let's just say there's a market and it can be exploited. Not a word to anyone else though. If I bring you into it, that's because you're an old friend and you're probably going to need the extra bread.'

'Take no notice of Alberto,' Cath said. 'He's always had his little side business as you know. I never ask questions, but it scares the hell out of me to tell you the truth.'

'One thing, Rick,' Alberto said, 'don't for Christ's sake spill the beans to Robert. He's got a big mouth, he'd probably write an article for the *Herald* about it.'

'Don't go on so much,' Cath said. 'Rick's got other problems on his mind at the moment.'

'Robert's all right,' Rick said. 'But don't worry, I remember something of his limitations. Anything for a good article.'

They drove through Miraflores and as they approached a plaza of brownish grass with a few bedraggled palm trees, Cathy pointed out their apartment block – white and rectangular. In the entrance they took the lift to the seventh floor. There Alberto who had the keys let them in. Rick saw at once that it was barely furnished. A double-bed in one bedroom, a single in another, a small gas-cooker in the kitchen. The living-room was empty. Dust and debris covered the parquet floor. The large windows were about three-feet from the floor and there was a sheer drop to a walled-in collection of shanties that stood next to a modern villa with a swimming-pool. In the distance he could see the copper foothills rashed with shanties. A greyish mist hung over the city to his left.

'Great apartment, Rick,' Alberto said. 'Fine views. Come round to the patio, you can see the ocean and the islands in the bay from that side.'

'You'll soon get it organised,' Cathy said. 'You're lucky, apartments are getting harder and harder to come by.'

Suddenly Rick felt utterly exhausted and besieged by doubts as to the wisdom of their move. As soon as Jean arrived, Cathy and Alberto who were anxious to leave made some arrangement to meet over the weekend. Alone with his wife, Rick put his arms around Jean.

'It's going to be all right,' she said. 'Once we've got everything sorted out.'

'Are you sure?'

'Of course, just don't worry.'

'There's a hell of a lot to do.'

'Well, let's put the children to bed and get a few hours sleep ourselves before we do anything else.'

The following day, Sunday, they had lunch at Robert and Sheila's, then went to the beach with Alberto and Cath. Things *had* changed, of course. Sheila was trying to persuade Robert to move to the States and it didn't take long to discover that Alberto and Cath's marriage was going through a bad patch. But that evening this was pushed into the background when Sara and Emma went down with an enteritis. They both had diarrhoea and both vomited frequently. On the Monday they were no better so Rick took them to a clinic recommended by Robert. The doctor, an elderly German with a mottled face and a brusque manner, advised their immediate hospitalisation. Rick spent the night at their bedside. Neither of the girls would eat or drink. An Indian nurse came every two hours to give them an injection.

'Unless we can persuade them to drink,' the doctor said, 'they could well die from dehydration. It's dangerous, this type of infection, dozens of babies die from it. Frankly I can't understand why you have brought your children to a rotten country like this.'

On the edge of panic Rick almost lost his temper, but stayed another twenty-four hours at the clinic. His daughters were still feverish. Through the long night he read them nursery rhymes when they were not sleeping. In the morning Jean called by. She'd been doing her best to fix up the apartment. She seemed quite calm. After discussing it with her, Rick took them out of the German clinic and went to the best pediatrician in Lima. He was Jewish and had been trained in the States. Reassuringly he told Rick to take his daughters home. He gave him a prescription for antibiotics.

'They'll survive,' he said.

That evening Delgado, the Director of the College, called round to find out why Rick hadn't started to work yet.

'The kids are sick and the flat is scarcely furnished,' he said. 'I need a week to help Jean get the place sorted out, then I'll start teaching.'

'But we need you now.'

'I'm sorry but it's out of the question. To tell you the truth I keep wondering whether we haven't made a mistake coming back here.'

'You've not been here a week yet,' Delgado said. 'Look, I want you to teach here so if it'll help, have a week off and get things straightened out. And if it's money that you're worried about I'm prepared to discuss a little extra on your salary.'

Paradise of Exiles

That week they bought some furniture and household necessities. Emma improved considerably although Sara still wasn't eating. She got rapidly thinner. Rick took her for walks round the district every afternoon and began to see the place through the distorting lens of his own disillusion. He felt he'd not seen the city clearly before. He noticed the religious slogans scrawled on the buses and taxis, *Vaya con Díos* and *El Amor de Díos*, conscious only of their irony. In the market Indian women with undernourished ragged children, whined for money. Rick was told that Indians actually celebrated the early death of their children in the belief that they would go straight to Heaven. On one occasion Delgado expressed a similar fatalism with regard to Rick's daughters. That night, lying in bed, he turned to Jean and buried his face between her breasts.

'I want to leave,' he said. 'I want to spend the money we've got for a second-hand car on our fares home.'

'Rick, we can't, not at this stage. It's going to be all right, really it is. Emma's eating normally again and I'm sure Sara will be fine soon. And when we've got that car and our stuff from England, it'll be good.'

'Everyone wanted us to come back, but they stay away when things are going badly. We've hardly seen a soul since that first weekend.'

'You're over-reacting, Rick,' she said. 'It's going to be all right.'

He held her tight and something in his manner touched her. He was usually so sure of himself, so confident, full of plans, full of nervous activity, rushing around meeting people while she hovered on the periphery. Now she realized how much he needed her and a small part of her mind resented the commitment this imposed upon her.

'Remember how much you loved it here,' she said. 'The beaches, those parties we used to have. It'll be the same again.'

'It's you and the children that are important to me.'

'But we'll enjoy ourselves her, I'm sure.'

'I still love you, you know, you must know that.'

'Make love to me then,' she said smiling.

He did so with an unaccustomed urgency and she smiled wryly to herself. Rick might appear tough enough to outsiders, but she knew his vulnerabilities. She knew that his social life was partly created to

23

disguise them and that when things went wrong he came running to her. In a way she was his sanctuary and because of it she felt the stronger. Rick needed to be liked, needed to feel loved. Too often he looked at people to find his own reflection and too rarely studied them for what they were. It was a blindness that could have led to self-destruction.

Rick lay back, lit a cigarette, exhaled. He was sweating slightly.

'Feel better?' Jean said laughing.

'Yes.'

He laughed too, the first time he'd laughed for days. Jean glanced down at his nakedness. His body was still slim and boyish. He didn't look thirty-four despite a few lines around his eyes. He hadn't changed much in the ten years she'd known him.

By that weekend Rick had started teaching and Sara was eating again. With the children convalescing he felt much better. Helped by Robert Redman he bought a second-hand Volkswagen. It cost more than he could really afford, but he went along to the British Institute and got evening classes three nights a week. His initial panic began to seem neurotic. With Cathy Morales he'd begun on some translations for an American magazine as well as *Ayllu*. And Alberto had offered to take him up to the north next time he went.

Rick was sitting in the sun on the patio of a white villa in the Rimac valley. He was sipping a gin-and-tonic, his fifth. On either side he could see the ochre foothills and below him the brown river winding through a corridor of emerald to the sea. He swirled the ice around the glass, lit a cigarette and watched Alberto playing with the children in the garden beneath him. The serrated Andean peaks were sharply outlined against the blue of the sky. In the sunlight their arid slopes were iridescent with the subtle mineral colours of the desert. Rick had an urge to drive on up the pass and down into the somnolent interior or beyond to where the mountains were covered in rain forest and tapering ravines corkscrewed out into the Amazon basin. Thousands of miles of uncharted jungle. The same sense of open space he felt in the hills.

That was the Peru he liked, not the city. He'd not come back to confront the injustices of the society though the difficulties he and Jean had been through made him question his motives for living there at all. They were dubious to say the least.

Alberto came up from the garden. He was sweating from his exertions. He took out his little packet of marijuana, rolled a joint and handed it to Rick.

'Have a smoke,' he said. 'It'll cheer you up. What's the matter these days anyway?'

'I'm still wondering whether I did the right thing coming back here, that's all.'

'You used to like it,' Alberto said. 'Take things as they come and don't worry so much.'

'Do you know why I came to Peru in the first place?'

'No idea. Why?'

'To escape the austerity and drabness of England in the fifties. I was deliberately seeking the exotic, I suppose.'

'What's the difference now?'

'It's changed in England now,' Rick said. 'A new mood of gaiety and freedom.' The marijuana was beginning to have its effect and he could feel himself becoming more expansive. 'Less of the old puritan ethos. Something exciting going on. As there seemed to be during the war.'

'Can you remember the war?'

'I was nearly five when it began. We were evacuated to a little mining-town in South Wales. We ran wild there.' He recalled daubing soot over the fences and pavements, getting lost in hills dotted with sheep, wandering round old slag heaps and pitstacks. 'We didn't stay long though. We returned just in time for the blitz. No one thought the war would last.'

'Did you see something of the bombing?'

'We slept in a shelter at the top of the garden and there were raids every night. Sometimes I'd creep outside to watch. It was like a firework display. Tracer bullets, searchlights, flak.' He had listened to the whine of bombs, the crackle of gunfire, the drone of planes, and in the morning afterwards had collected shrapnel, torn and jagged lumps of metal that he would swap for marbles at school.

'What about the hardship and shortage?'

'We were lucky, I suppose, but I really got the impression that there was a kind of excitement about. I can't remember feeling frightened. There was a sort of friendliness and energy.'

'I imagine you kids took the war pretty much for granted.'

'A normal part of childhood, yes, I suppose so.' Their street had straggled out in the country. There had been a wheatfield full of poppies at the back and a deserted farmhouse. In the village, a mile away, there was an old mansion locked up and festooned with barbed-wire which they'd broken into and come to regard as a playground. Beyond that was an ack-ack post and a cemetery with grey crosses above grassy mounds. His grandmother was buried there and he used to go with his father to trim the grass. Afterwards they would climb up the Saxon tumulus or go down to the river and watch the water-rats scurrying into holes on the far bank.

'Didn't anyone close to you, any relative, get killed?'

'I don't think so. I remember getting a bit scared when we first heard about the flying bombs.' He had enjoyed listening to scraps of news on the wireless and reading about the various campaigns. And he'd learnt to hate the Nazi leaders, hate the mention of their names.

Jean and Cathy came over to their table with drinks. They said that lunch was almost ready.

'He's been telling me about World War II,' Alberto said laughing. 'I didn't realize he was old enough to remember it.'

After lunch Cathy took them further up the valley to meet the poet and publisher, Javiér Eguren. He lived in a sort of writers' colony near Chosica. A shy yet charming man he seemed to know almost everyone in the Lima literary-world and for Cath was an invaluable source of information, possessing every book of poetry ever published in Peru. She and Jean spent the afternoon talking to him and browsing through his library while Alberto and Rick sat outside in the sun, stoned, drinking *pisco* sours, keeping an eye on the children.

In the early evening Julio Scorza appeared. Rick was anxious to meet him. He'd heard a lot about him from Cathy and recently Julio had criticised some translations they'd published in *Ayllu*.

'I hope you found my review constructive,' he said when someone brought up the subject.

'I thought it was most unfair,' Cath said.

'I wrote it with the best of intentions.'

'I'm sure you did.'

'Don't take any notice of Julio,' Eguren said. 'He puts everyone down at some time or another. It's his own insecurity.'

'I'd like a copy of your recent book anyway,' Rick said.

'You surprise me. Out of loyalty to Cath I'd imagined you would just want to stab me in the back, metaphorically-speaking.'

'When it comes to poetry I try to be objective,' Rick said. 'And I'd like to translate some of your new poems. I liked those we've done already.'

'Well, I'd like to see your versions before they're actually published.'

'We could go over them together.'

'Let's meet soon then,' Julio said. 'I'd like to find out whether or not we're on the same wavelength. Which poets have influenced you, for instance?'

'I'm afraid my influences are mainly American.'

'Why *afraid*? I'm no lover of the good old U.S. of A, but I can be dispassionate when it comes to poetry too and some of the most interesting poets over the last few years have undoubtedly been American. It's a strange country. It seems to produce some of the best things in this world and also some of the worst, by God!'

'You could be right.'

'I'm sure I'm right,' Julio said. 'I'll put a copy of my new book in the post. Possibly we could arrange to meet at Robert's. He's a good friend of mine though he knows little about poetry.'

'Do you play chess?'

'Of course.'

'We'll have a few games then.'

'Good idea.'

'The trouble with Julio,' Cath said the moment he had left, 'is that he confuses poetry with ego-tripping. It's a competitive game to him.'

'He's the best poet I've come across here,' Rick said.

'I suppose he is,' Cathy said. 'Just don't you tell him I said so.'

The evening was still warm, but as the children were getting tired, whining for more Coca Cola, Jean and Cath decided it was time to go. Eguren and his wife helped them collect their things together and Alberto loaded them into the VW. They said goodbye and drove off to join the long convoy of Sunday traffic heading back for the city.

Robert Redman was hurrying along Jirón Unión towards Plaza de Armas. For his next assignment, the editor of the *Herald* had just told him, he had to go to Cuzco. The prospect of the trip excited him. So did the narrow crowded street which at this time of the evening seemed to generate an erotic aura. Before he'd met Sheila it had been a regular haunt of his. He used to watch the honey-skinned *mestiza* girls coming out of offices and shops, hurrying off, he imagined, to clandestine dates, or dashing into one of the old churches for a quick tryst with God. To kneel in front of altars smothered in jewels and set in gold leaf or gaze at the garishly-painted ikons of a tortured Christ, to confess some small sin or beg for some small favour. Occasionally he had waited for some particularly attractive girl, knowing that she would probably emerge smiling and flirtatious, ready to accept the offer of a drink or dinner. Religion and sex were inextricably inter-related in Lima. Or was that only in his fantasies?

He passed an Indian woman selling *anticuchos* which she grilled over a small brazier. The smell of garlic and oil hung in the air. At another stall a man was selling beads and images of the local saint, Martín de Porres. Momentarily Robert recalled the catacombs in San Francisco which were piled high with yellowed bones, skulls and bits of shrivelled cassock, dusty old shrouds and habits, the damp smell of mould and decay.

He reached the end of Unión where a bowler-hatted Indian woman was rummaging through the rubbish in a bin. A couple of freelance whores smiled at him as they passed and the whole of the square in front was pinkish in the glow of sunset. The fountain in the centre of the plaza was surrounded by the usual shoeshine boys and Robert caught sight of the goose-stepping guards in front of the President's palace. As he crossed, running the gauntlet of the beggars, he saw the scarlet flash of a cardinal bird in the palms and almost at the same instant Sheila's long blonde hair as she sat at a pavement-cafe, the Versailles, next to the gigantic statue of Pizarro. He sat down beside her and ordered a Coca Cola.

'We're going to Cuzco,' he said.

'Great, but why?'

'I've got to interview some priest who's been annoying the authorities, preaching revolution from the pulpit or something. They're paying my expenses so if we stay at a cheap hotel we'll have enough to visit Machu Picchu.'

'When are we going?'

'Sometime next week.'

Sheila had certainly changed his life, Robert thought, sipping his Coke, though he had no regrets about that. When she'd first phoned him up he was one of the editors of *Ayllu*. He had taken her to dinner and during it offered to publish some of her poems. Before he could actually do so he had resigned from the magazine after quarrelling with Cathy Morales, but their affair had begun by then. When Sheila wanted to move out of the pensión where she had been staying, Robert invited her to share his flat. She'd been there ever since. It amused him that she had once been a *novice*, for him it had given the relationship a special piquancy, but it was on a weekend trip to Tingo Maria that he'd come to realize he loved her. Now he saw those three days as a turning-point.

'I'd like another beer,' Sheila said. 'Why don't you have one?'

'Rick and Jean are coming round later so I don't want to be too long. There's this science-fiction film in Miraflores. We might all go and see it.'

'How about eating out? Then we could go to the late show. We could take them to Pio Pio.' It was their favourite restaurant, specialising in barbecued chicken and salad.

'If they pay for themselves.'

'Don't be so mean,' Sheila said. 'They're hard up at the moment.' She was smiling. Robert's tendency to be tight with money had long been a joke between them. It too had started that weekend in Tingo Maria. Knowing that Robert had had to go, she virtually invited herself. He agreed, provided they shared expenses. This he did to the letter, even to a division of their bar bills. It had amused Sheila and oddly endeared him to her.

'You're a bit of a tight-ass,' she'd said, half-admiringly.

They had stayed at a rambling wooden hotel with a rusty-coloured corrugated-iron roof and a long balcony from which they could watch the river flowing below them, the sound of pebbles rolled along its bed like thousands of marbles in a huge bag. They bought boots and machetes, then explored the fringe of jungle, hacking a way through, wading a shallow stream and getting bogged down in swamp. When Robert took what he thought was a short-cut to the hotel they got lost and finally arrived back dripping with sweat, covered in insect bites, exhausted. They took a shower together, then made love under the mosquito netting. Afterwards, sitting on the balcony and sipping a cold beer while the sun set, it had all seemed very romantic.

Sheila not only tackled that expedition, but every other one on which he'd taken her, with the *sang-froid* he'd come to expect only from a man. In the high Andes on the bus journey back to Lima, the landscape bleak and forbidding, snow fluttering in the intensely cold wind, she gave him her poncho when he started to shiver.

'She saved my life that night,' he told his friends back in the city.

Chapter Three

Alberto was having a drink in the Corsega, a small bar a few blocks from Plaza San Martín. It was nine o'clock and he'd just driven into the city from the hatchery. He thought of inviting Rick for a drink, then remembered that he'd promised Cath he would be home early. The promise itself irritated him. He felt that she had extracted it by a species of blackmail. Had she not done so he might well have gone home in time to take her out somewhere. The previous evening he had stayed in, bored, morose and mildly restless while Cathy had worked for hours on some translations for her goddamn magazine. The thought of this decided him. He wouldn't go home yet. He'd have another beer. He felt like lighting up a joint but supposed it would be too risky here.

Two men were eating at a table and in the shadows on the far side a girl sipped a Coke. When Alberto went up to get another beer she smiled at him and he recognised her. It was Monica, a small thin girl he'd often danced with at the Golden Gate. He invited her to have a drink. She asked for a whiskey and began questioning him about mutual acquaintances.

'What about Roberto? Have you seen him recently?'

'Saw him in the Zanzibar the other week.'

'Was he with that American, *la rubia*?'

'Yes.'

'Are they married yet?'

'Just living together.'

'The same thing,' she said. 'He used to be a friend of mine.'

Alberto smiled, finished his beer and ordered another. Monica had another whiskey. She had an animated little face and the pixie-sized body of a pubescent girl.

31

'*Ya me voy*,' she said when she'd finished her drink.

'So early?'

'A friend of mine advised me to stay at home tonight. He said there was going to be trouble.'

'He was probably joking.'

'No, he's a lieutenant in the army.'

'I know there have been riots in the provinces and unrest here, but that's normal.'

'He sounded pretty sure of himself. Why don't you get some whiskey and come back to my place?'

'I'm short of cash.'

'Two hundred *soles*, that's all.'

'I wouldn't have that much if I bought some whiskey, but we don't need it, I've got some grass.'

'Let's go then.'

Alberto hesitated a moment, but he needed a joint and at least he could have one in the privacy of Monica's pad. He would stay a while then drive back to San Isidro.

There were a few people about outside, but the streets seemed comparatively deserted for that time of night. Monica's flat was on the thirteenth floor of a nearby building. It was clean and spacious with a wide low bed, a couple of easy chairs, some Peruvian rugs over the parquet floor and a small adjacent bathroom. Alberto went over to the window. He could see the rectangles of street-lamps radiating from the plaza, the huge Coca Cola advert in red-and-blue neon flashing on and off, and the lights of the Hotel Bolivar. Over to his right was San Cristóbal, its yellow-lit cross almost disembodied as the hill itself blended into the darkness.

He turned back to the room. Monica was wrapped in a blue kimono. Alberto took out his little packet of marijuana and rolled a cigarette in his machine. He lit it, inhaled and passed it to Monica. She inhaled, coughed and gave it back to him.

'Have you got any music?' he asked.

She turned on her radio, twiddling the dials until she found some jazz. The reception was poor. Crackles and harsh clipped voices rattling away in rapid Spanish interfered with the music. There was some scrambled morse, a few more squeaks and high-pitched buzzes, then a folk song played by a local band.

'Turn it off,' Alberto said. He went across to Monica, put his arm out to her, noticing as she smiled the glint of a gold-filling. Her lips didn't part when he kissed her, but remained hard. And he caught a whiff of garlic on her breath.

'Have you got two hundred?'

He took some notes from his back pocket and gave her the money. Standing together she came just below the level of his shoulders and amused him when she led him quite forcefully to the bed. She could only have been half his weight.

Lying on the bed she immediately began to touch him with small knowing fingers, dark brown against the whiteness of his body. He felt fat beside her. Perhaps he'd go to the gymnasium the following day. He could do with losing some weight. Monica had turned off the light and the room was pervaded by pale reflections from the neons outside. Feeling lazy Alberto pulled Monica on top of him. A featherweight, she straddled him lightly. Alberto was amused by the incongruous position, her childlike quick-moving body bobbing above his lap, but she soon tired and switched positions. Beneath him she felt fragile and angular, but soft-skinned.

When they had finished he smoked another joint and gradually became aware of an alien noise outside. It was the harsh chanting of distant voices. Then from a loudspeaker or megaphone a grating voice making some speech. He went to the window. In the plaza a crowd had gathered beneath the plinth of San Martín's statue. Someone was standing upon it, shouting. Alberto could make out several banners among the crowd. On one he could just about read the words. They seemed absurd in the circumstances: VIVA EL PERU CAMPEON MUNDIAL DE FUTBOL.

'It's some sort of demonstration,' he said.

At that moment a scuffle erupted and he watched a cordon of armed police converge upon the plaza. The shouting grew louder and the crowd began to move towards the Colmena, the police following.

'I told you there would be trouble tonight,' Monica said. The shouting grew louder and Alberto thought he heard the sharp crack of rifle shots though they could have been firecrackers. Absorbed by the spectacle beneath him he saw in it too the perfect excuse, an alibi.

'Are you on the phone here?'

Monica pointed to it and he went over and dialled Cathy's number. She sounded weary enough, but not too upset when he explained that there was trouble in the city, a demonstration against the government or something. He would return home as soon as it was safe. She told him she had been over to Rick's to work on the contributors' notes for *Ayllu*. She felt worn out and was off to bed. 'Yes,' she added in answer to his final question, 'the kids are fine – they are sleeping.' Alberto felt tired himself. Behind the mild euphoria induced by the marijuana was a pleasant languor. He got back into bed beside Monica, pulled up the sheet and soon dozed off.

He was aroused from a vivid dream by an odd rumbling sound. He looked at his watch. It was gone three o'clock. Monica was sitting up in bed. From outside came the continuous harsh noise that had woken them. At first Alberto thought it was the onset of a tremor, then realized it was produced by moving vehicles. Once more he went to the window. Below him the black sinister shapes of tanks and armoured cars were rolling towards the plaza. In between came trucks packed with the dark still figures of soldiers, their weapons reflecting the glint of the odd street-light. Other soldiers were marching along the pavement, rifles held at the ready.

'Something's going on now all right,' he said. 'Looks like a full-scale military operation.'

'*Madre mia!*' Monica said joining him at the window.

'I must go,' Alberto said. He had a mental picture of himself stranded all night at Monica's and having to explain to Cath in the morning.

'*Ahora?*'

'Yes.'

'Be careful then.'

On the ground floor he waited for a moment. Through the swing doors he saw that the street was empty, but he could still hear the rumble of the tanks, and then abruptly came the sound of automatic fire, shouts, a single scream. On the Colmena it looked clear except for one or two hurrying civilians in the same situation as himself.

Cautiously and keeping well into the shadows, Alberto jogged towards the street off the plaza where he had left his VW. He wondered if it would still be there.

Passing the Negro-negro he spotted Julio Scorza standing in the doorway with a couple of friends. As the centre of Lima was always a bit like a village he was only mildly surprised. Julio was smiling broadly.

'It's come,' he said. 'The revolution. Let's have a beer and celebrate.'

'What's happened?'

'The army's taken over. I watched the whole scene, man, it was certainly well-planned.'

'Is it safe in the streets?'

'I think so. No one knows much about it yet. There won't be any reaction until the press puts out the news in the morning.'

'What was that demonstration last night?'

'Oh that. Nothing much. The police dispersed it.'

'Did you know things were going to happen?'

'There have been lots of rumours,' Julio said. 'Let's go into Miraflores and have a beer there.'

'I've got my car if it's still where I parked it.'

'Great.'

The car was untouched. They got in.

'They're supposed to be socialists, these rebel officers,' Julio said. 'I reckon they'll make a few changes. Nationalise some of the foreign companies to start with. Shuffle up the civil service . . .'

Alberto swung the car round and proceeded down Jirón Camaná, but within a hundred yards there was a road-block. An armoured truck was parked sideways across the narrow street. As Alberto approached, two soldiers ran out and halted them. They walked menacingly towards the VW, their short black automatic weapons pointing at the car.

'Where are you going?'

'Trying to get home,' Alberto said.

'Not this way, you'll have to try Avenida Wilson. My advice is to get indoors as soon as you can. A curfew has already been imposed.'

'We were having a drink in town.'

'Then go home now. It's dangerous here.'

Alberto did a three-point turn and drove back to the Colmena, reaching Avenida Arequipa by a circuitous route. As they sped along the wide avenue into Miraflores Julio talked continuously. He was elated and optimistic about the *coup d'etat*, its future effect upon the country. Alberto said little. He was anxious about his parents' business and his other activities. He wanted to go up to the north again soon, to Ecuador this time, and he had been hoping to take Rick with him. He liked the country as it was and wanted to carry on in his own sweet way as long as possible. The only excitement he felt was in having witnessed the event.

Rick was having a shower before going to work when Robert Redman called. It was seven-thirty and Robert was bubbling with excitement. He burst into the bathroom where Rick was drying himself, followed by Jean.

'There's no school for you today,' he said grinning.

'I thought you were supposed to be in Cuzco.'

'The trip's been cancelled. There's been a revolution.'

'You're joking.'

'The *Herald* phoned me up at six this morning. They want me to go into the city and find out exactly what's happening. A group of colonels has taken over. The army, tanks and all, swarmed into Lima last night, soldiers got into the palace, arrested the President and put him on a flight to Buenos Aires. It must have been hilarious.'

'Hilarious?'

'He stripped the colonels of their rank! Then they bundled him off, protesting all the way to the airport.'

'What's going to happen?'

'Military dictatorship, Rick. National socialism.'

'You mean fascism?'

'Not exactly no. These colonels may have studied at military academies in the States, but they got their ideals from Cuba.'

'It sounds complicated.'

'One thing's certain – there will be censorship of the press now. That's why I want to get my article in first. They're sure to attack foreign journalists, especially those who criticise the revolution.'

Paradise of Exiles

'How will it affect me?'

'Not at all, I imagine, not unless they take over the private colleges. But I could be in trouble, I've written a few harsh things about this country in the past.'

'I thought the circulation of the *Herald* was limited to the British community.'

'They still might have me down for deportation. I might go to the States anyway. I shall if things get sticky or I lose my job. But right now I'm going into Lima to see what's going on. Do you want to come?'

'Of course.'

'I wouldn't if I were you,' Jean said.

'Can't miss a revolution.'

'Well,' she said, 'for God's sake, be careful.'

Outside mist and low cloud hung over the entire city. Even the foothills were invisible. Rick drove cautiously into the centre and parked in a sidestreet. There were few people about, but as the two men walked towards Plaza San Martín they could hear shouting, the sporadic crackle of automatic fire and the guttural voice of an official over some loudspeaker system. The plaza was full of people, some climbing up on the gigantic plinth upon which San Martín sat astride his monumental horse. Rick knew the words engraved upon that plinth: Liberty, Equality, Justice. Few people read them, of course, and on normal days only the bootblacks used the plinth. Stray dogs would sometimes piss against it and beggars occasionally slept in its shadow, but now it was milling with demonstrators.

'What's the bloke with the megaphone saying?'

'I can't catch it,' Robert said. 'Something about everyone going home and staying indoors.'

Just then they caught sight of tanks emerging from the three streets that branched off the square. The squat green vehicles halted and their guns swung like antennae towards the statue. Behind them marched platoons of green-uniformed brown-faced soldiers. They halted and began to fan out round three sides of the plaza, rifles unslung, bayonets fixed. There were shouts and jeers from the phalanx of students in the centre. Several stones were thrown. They bounced on the tarmac and

37

clattered on the steel-plated sides of the tanks. Rick heard the sound of breaking glass and saw one of the soldiers suddenly double up, his hand against his face.

'There'll be real trouble now,' Robert said.

A handful of soldiers, ran half-crouching towards the plaza and hurled smoking objects towards it. A couple of army trucks began to move forward.

'They're going to turn on the hosepipes,' Robert said. 'Let's get out.'

They backed away as powerful jets of white carved great corridors through the crowd. People began to scatter. A few braver ones were running towards the ominously still and silent tanks; others towards the soldiers at the far end of their fan. Automatic fire broke out from various angles. Rick saw the flash of orange, heard the staccato explosion of shots. At that moment everyone began to run. Robert and Rick ran too. Most of the bullets shrilled over the heads of the crowd, but running close to the wall opposite the Hotel Bolivar, Rick saw chunks of plaster ripped from the side of the building at shoulder-height just in front of him.

'Get down,' he yelled and flung himself flat. Robert did the same. Bursts of fire continued. Several bodies were lying at unnatural angles in the street.

'I know someone who lives in the next block down,' Robert said. 'If we can reach it, we'll be safe.'

The street was full of running people as they started on their weaving sprint. Rick glanced behind him. A hundred yards away the soldiers were coming in a line across the street. They seemed to have stopped shooting. Robert reached the block of flats. Rick dived after him through the unlocked swing doors. Near the lift Robert rang one of the bells on the intercom. The voice that answered sounded anxious, suspicious, then Rick heard a short laugh.

'We can go up,' Robert said.

They got in the lift and were wafted to the thirteenth floor. Robert rang the bell of a door to their left. Monica let them in.

'*Que tal?*'

'Fine, but out of breath,' Robert said.

'Your friend, Alberto, was here earlier. He came back for a drink last night and had to stay.'

Rick went straight to the window. Below citizens and soldiers were still running about. He could hear the sound of shots, shouts, the rumble of tanks.

'Well, you've got your story,' he said.

'I was scared stiff, weren't you?'

Monica came from the kitchenette with coffee. She couldn't remember Rick, but he recognised her from evenings at the Golden Gate a year or two before. They stayed with her for a couple of hours, watching the troops clear the streets. They witnessed a number of arrests and saw at least three people either killed or seriously wounded taken away by ambulance. By midday with the city in the control of the military, people were beginning to carry on with their normal activities. And they were able to leave.

That evening when Rick and Jean arrived at the Haiti it was already crowded. Julio Scorza was there with a girl he introduced as Ana-Maria. Rick recognised her as a student of his at the British Institute. They were sitting at a table with Robert and Sheila. Rick joined them and ordered beers all round. Not long after that Alberto and Cathy came in. Everyone seemed to be talking at once, but most of it felt speculative and academic after the events of the morning.

'It's probably the best thing that's happened to this country for a long time,' Julio said.

'But there's going to be a dictatorship,' Rick said.

'We've had years of exploitation by foreign companies on the one hand and the oligarchy on the other. The army will change all that.'

'I don't for a moment believe it will,' Alberto said.

'It's just an interim government,' Julio said. 'It's the first stage of revolution. It'll pave the way for the Marxists later.'

'Remember what Bolivar once said?' Cathy asked.

'What?'

'Those who ploughed the revolution, ploughed the sea.'

'That was a hundred-and-fifty years ago.'

'History repeats itself as you yourself have so often said. We've just replaced one rule, that of the rich, for another even more repressive, the army.'

'And after three years in the army I can tell you something about it,' Alberto said. 'Its justice is arbitrary, its system hierarchical and its sense of individual freedom practically nil.'

'You're all pessimistic,' Julio said. '*Gringos* who don't really want any change. You're part of the status quo and you're doing well here because of it.'

'Were there any casualties?' Jean asked.

'According to official sources there was only one,' Robert told her. 'A sixteen-year old boy.'

'Shot through the eye,' Cathy added. 'He died in hospital this afternoon.'

'It's not that I don't believe there should be change,' Rick said to Julio. 'I'm just sceptical of dictatorships.'

'It's only a first step,' Julio said. 'You'll see.'

As the others were talking Rick thought of the journey he took every day to college. Yellow buses made in the States roared up the dual carriage-way towards the foothills. They passed irrigated farmland, clusters of shanties and the new racetrack. Outside the huts there were always a few Indian women picking lice out of their children's hair and ragged boys herding goats along the grass verge. Men would already be at work in the cotton fields; others selling fruit at the junction with the Pan-American highway. And the students in the buses, children of the wealthy, always seemed oblivious of such scenes. They were more interested in the flashy cars that overtook them or in the peacocks that fluttered away as their bus turned into the college gates.

In his office off Plaza San Martín Robert was reading a letter he'd received from a secretary at the Ministry of Information. 'The military government,' it said, 'valued a sympathetic and constructive approach to the revolution, but would be obliged to censor all articles in future if they contained destructive criticism.' Robert smiled to himself, surprised that his article should have merited any attention at all. He wondered whether he would get fired, or at least a rocket from his editor. He got a copy of the *Herald* from his file.

'The military have inaugurated a wave of puritanism,' he'd written. 'They describe it themselves as a morality campaign, but it seems to be concerned only with minor trends such as the wearing of miniskirts, the growing use of soft drugs, and pop-music. There has been much talk in the official press of decadence and corruption in society along with a new emphasis upon National Dignity and Sovereignty, whatever such terms mean. However, it will be difficult to assess the true nature of the new regime in the forthcoming weeks as independent opinion is slowly, but surely being muzzled . . .'

Chapter Four

Everywhere he went there were churches. Old, crumbling, colonial. A feast for tourists and a hazard during earthquakes. On their facades were gargoyles, cherubims and angels, some of worm-eaten wood, others of plaster and stone. They were a-sexual with grimacing faces or coy smiles, perched above the city, halfway as it were between heaven and earth. Julio's favourite church was that of Santa Rosa, partly because of the legends that abounded about the saint herself. Out of some mystical darkness she had prophesied the doom of Lima. It would be destroyed by a terrible earthquake. She'd seen the masts of galleons in the Plaza de Armas several miles from the coast carried there on a tidal wave. And thousands of people believed that one day her vision would materialise.

'The poor bloody masochist,' he'd say aloud everytime he passed her church. But perhaps she was right. The city would be obliterated. Someday waves of shanty-dwellers would descend upon it from their encampments in the suburbs. Like Rome the city was besieged by barbarian hordes though few of its citizens seemed aware of it. The vandals were at the gates, the foothills black with their tents and inside the walls politicians and bureaucrats fiddled like Nero. Fiddled and cheated and conned to feather their own nests. Blind to reality and the imminent holocaust, they paid no heed to the warnings of their prophets. His own book of poems, a prophetic-enough vision of the dangers, had sold a mere 431 copies and merited two complacent reviews in the press.

He went into the Versailles and ordered a large beer. He had been doing the rounds of the cafes and was already a little drunk. His extravagant pessimism was a result of this and some recent disillusionment with the military government. Could it be that his foreign companions were right though for the wrong reasons? He thought of Rick Preston, his scepticism, and on an impulse decided to visit him. The other week he'd gone over Preston's translations of his poems which were to be published in *Ayllu*. They were good, better than he had expected. Idiomatic, racy even, but then English was a language suited to their tone. Since then he had got hold of some of Preston's own poems. They were readable and direct, with little poetic embellishment or wilful obscurity, but rather too personal perhaps. Lacking in intellectual force which was odd because Preston played a good game of chess. In a certain mood Julio enjoyed playing the game – the intellectual excitement when your opponent was outwitted.

He finished his beer and left the Versailles. Preston also had an attractive wife and as Ezra Pound had once said: it was restful to be among beautiful women. He caught a taxi to Miraflores and as they were cruising along Avenida Arequipa checked his address-book. Within twenty minutes he was outside the Preston's apartment block. Jean answered the bell. Rick had gone up to the north with Alberto Morales, she said, but invited him in for a coffee.

Out of politeness he stayed about half-an-hour, making desultory conversation and browsing along Preston's bookshelves. Jean was busy getting her three children to bed and Julio always felt uneasy in the company of sticky-fingered toddlers with their endless curiosity and demands for attention. Mothers with children in tow were far from restful. He borrowed a couple of books by American poets, excused himself and left. He walked back into Miraflores and ended up at the cinema. Fellini's *La Dolce Vita* was showing. It suited his mood entirely.

While Rick and Alberto were on their trip to Ecuador, Jean and Cath drove to Punta Hermosa and the beach. It was fine weather, early summer. The highway curved south out of the city through the Lurín valley, yellow and green with cotton and rice in startling contrast to the pyramid-shaped foothills rising to the Andes. They passed the pre-Incaic shrine, Pachacamac, and the nearby reconstructed monastery for Virgins of the Sun. Jean felt exhilarated. Out in the Pacific she could see the off-shore islands shaped like a whale's back, glinting amber in the sunlight. She watched a pair of buzzards hovering over the ruins and up the valley could see a puff of powder-blue – the jacaranda trees in blossom. She was glad Rick had gone north; his depressions had begun to get her down. She felt a sense of freedom, alone with the children, and for the hundredth time that year contemplated the possibility of separation when they returned to England.

She still loved him, yes, but he was so difficult to live with. It had taken her long enough to realize this and to realize too that he needed her more than she needed him. In certain ways at least. She knew she could manage her own life satisfactorily. Rick she felt could not. He was so irresponsible, so impulsive, such a bad judge of character. He got involved with the most stupid people, especially women. Invariably they were neurotic and confused like himself. Which was probably why they were drawn to him. It was true that since their return he'd been, so far as she knew, completely faithful, but that was simply because of the bad patch they'd been through. Rick liked to think he'd changed. She knew he had not, not deeply. At one time his drinking bouts and affairs had filled her with despair. Not now. They simply bored her.

Cathy turned off the highway and drove down a dusty track that sloped steeply to the beach. It was Jean's favourite bay, El Silencio, horseshoe-shaped, deserted in the week, the sea dark blue, vivid against the ochre cliffs and greyish sand. They went to the far end, changed the children, stretched out on ponchos and relaxed in the sun. Cath, whose constant complaints about Alberto had sparked off Jean's train of thought, returned to the attack now. It obsessed her these days. She could talk of little else.

'Do you know *exactly* what they're doing up in the north?' she asked.

'Yes, getting some marijuana.'

'But do you know how dangerous that is? If they're caught it would be a prison sentence as well as a fine. And you know what prison means here?'

'Well, frankly I'm enjoying the peace.'

'So am I. But it makes me sick, especially Alberto. He really doesn't give a damn. He goes off for a week at a time and comes home as if nothing had happened. Oh I know he's not with another woman – I'd prefer it if he was, I think. He's smoking grass and listening to pop music, wasting his talents. He's intelligent, you know. He could do anything he wanted, but, no, he just doesn't care. Money doesn't worry him in the slightest. He's always been rescued by his parents. They're wealthy. They own land. But Alberto doesn't. He's just inherited the playboy mentality. Flying a plane, chasing all over the country for drugs. Says he loves me and the kids, but hardly ever spends any time with us.'

'He's always charming when he comes round to see us. And generous.'

'Sure he's charming. He can talk the hindleg off a mule. And he's generous because he doesn't care about money. That's the trouble. But he's in a world of his own, a fantasy. He says he's going to be rich one day, but he'll never be unless he changes. He lacks the stamina, the will-power, to work hard at anything.'

'Well, most of the men I know seem to be much the same,' Jean said, a little embarrassed by Cath's disloyalty.

'Rick's all right,' Cath said. 'At least he has ambition. He wants to achieve something. He's home with you most of the time. And he works.'

Jean laughed. 'You don't know him, Cath. It's women that are his weakness.'

'I know that, I'd rather Alberto were the same way. Besides, Rick doesn't seem to have spent much time running around after women this year.'

'No, when things are going badly for him he does a moral turnabout. As soon as things are going well he'll be the same as ever.'

'Well, I'll tell you something, Jean. Unless Alberto bucks up a bit I'm leaving him. I can't stand the lack of security, the skating from one crisis to another. I'm going to take the kids and go back to the States.'

'Come on,' Jean said. 'Let's have a swim and enjoy ourselves while they're away.' She laughed and strolled down towards the sea, followed by Cath and the six naked children. 'Trouble is I miss Rick,' Jean said. 'I miss him when he's away. He's so vulnerable really. And he needs so much comforting. Worse than the children.'

'I feel the same about Alberto, but I'm getting harder every time he comes and cries on my shoulder and wants reassurance. I don't intend to go on mothering him for the rest of my life.'

'That's it,' Jean said. 'They're just like babies. Let me know when you're off to the States. I might just come with you.'

She laughed again and dived into the breaker, coming up the other side, the water green, cool to her suntanned skin. She swam out through a scum of shells, seaweed, dead fish. Close in to the shore the water was brackish with debris. She shuddered as she bobbed against a dead bird, black and white wings, the thin blue spears of its bill, then emerged into clear water. Under the surface it was lime green, opaque, with grains of coarse sand swirling around her. Just beyond the next breaker she caught sight of a black fin. Her belly went weak with alarm. Then she saw the curve of a black back. A porpoise. They often came into the bay. Harmless, though Jean didn't like being in the water with them. She swam back to the beach. Cath had seen the porpoise too. They watched three of them, their dorsal fins furrowing through the waves.

Jean lay back on the poncho, her body drying in the sun, while Cath took the children for a walk along the beach. The sun's weight felt heavy on her shoulders. She flipped out a hand and found a shell, playing with it. The wind was blowing sandwich-papers along the beach. She could hear the sea roaring in front of her with a kind of menace. Then she glanced back towards the cliffs. Ropes of sand were swirling down and beyond were the stone-blind mountains . . . Quite suddenly she recalled the tenement in Birmingham where she had lived for eighteen years. Its walls had been beer-bottle brown and glassy with damp, its stone passages always moist. A squalid place. And her father, like an urban gypsy, always out of work, often drunk, once in prison for some petty felony. During the War he used to loot bombed-sites. Sometimes he'd beat her mother. And now he was dead of cancer. Jean wondered whether she had inherited the same weakness. Her father had always seemed so strong and yet all the time his cells must have been running riot in his body, his chemistry going haywire. Her father's death had obsessed her recently, because she'd always thought of him as a survivor. And cancer, fear of those rebelling cells, that potential within her, made her feel momentarily cold despite the sun.

Those first eighteen years had been a period of poverty. Jean had been forced to leave school at fourteen and get a job as a shop-assistant. She'd worked in the ceramic department of a store in the city and studied art, literature and languages at night-school, determined to get out of the rut. A deprived childhood, she supposed, but rich enough in many ways. She remembered her grandfather in his scarlet-and-black dress-uniform. Just before the War that was. He kept pigeons in his spare time and used to call them down with a rattling whistle from the loft on the roof of the flats. And her grandmother whose hair had always been white and who drank too much Guinness. Considered crazy by the rest of the family, she wrote terrible novelettes which she kept in notebooks. They had titles such as *The Drunkard's Bride*. When Jean had read them she had felt the anger running through, though the language failed to create anything but melodrama. Now she too was dead. Of TB in a home for old-age pensioners. And her grandfather – of a heart-attack while washing at the kitchen sink.

Out of the blue, with (in fact) his blue eyes and brown hair, Rick had appeared. He picked her up at the store where she worked. With his talk of poetry, his anecdotes about travel, his air of candour, his quick smile and slow soft voice, he'd seemed like a knight-errant. Within a week or two she found her regular boyfriend, Gilbert, boring. Two weeks after they met he made love to her. She'd taken no persuading. She'd never wanted anyone in the same way before. And she felt she'd hung on to her virginity too long. She was twenty then. Rick, she thought, had *seduced* her with his ambition to be a writer and his worldly experience which had seemed extensive then.

She smiled to herself and wondered what life would have been like had she married Gilbert. With his gentle brown eyes, his bicycle and his patience, he had seen himself as her protector. He played football on Sundays, went to the local with the lads twice a week and worked as a clerk at the Town Hall. He didn't make love to her. He believed, as they were told to in those days, in waiting for marriage. He had wanted to get married. He wanted babies. He wanted a normal respectable life in a middle-class suburb. And Jean had rejected all that. Because as much as she'd liked Gilbert as a friend she wasn't excited by him. Rick didn't want marriage. He scoffed at the idea of it. He wanted to be famous. He wanted to travel. He wanted Jean. To make love to her as often as possible.

So she'd chosen Rick and never for a moment doubted the wisdom of that choice. Never imagined it would turn out the way it had. For a year in Birmingham they'd gone out together while Rick had one job after another. They made out every night. At Rick's parents' if they were out. At her parents' place after they'd gone to bed. On the floor in front of the dying embers of a coal-fire. Outside in the woods and fields if there was nowhere else. And once, she remembered, on their coats when a few inches of snow covered the ground. They only had one serious quarrel. When Rick took out a girl he'd known a year or so before. Jean had finished with him. Rick had gone hitch-hiking round Europe for a month with his brother. When he'd called round on the night of his return, thin and suntanned, with a fading black-eye from some fight, saying how much he'd missed her, that he knew now he loved her and wanted to marry her, she'd forgiven him his betrayal because it seemed absurd.

'I love you, Jean.' That was what he'd said and she would have done anything for him, gone anywhere with him, followed him to the metaphorical corners of the globe. In fact they went down to London. Got married and lived in a coldwater flat. But it hadn't mattered to Jean. Rick had a dozen jobs and got fired from most of them. He wrote in his spare time. They walked all over Highgate and Hampstead, made love in the big old-fashioned bed with the brass knobs on the headpiece, and Jean was happier than she'd ever been before.

What had happened, then, over the last few years? For now she was dissatisfied. She knew Rick better and had less patience with him. She had grown up, she thought wryly, and yet in a way she felt more tied to him than ever. She could leave him. They could separate. But she'd always be linked to him. Not just because of the children either, but because of what they'd shared together. The emotional traumas they'd been through. And, she supposed, most couples were the same in that way.

She looked at Cathy by her side, smoking a cigarette. Her eyes were closed. She too was lost in some acid burrow of despair. Jean scraped up some sand. Like basalt, crystal, quartz. Shells that splintered like sugar. A cockle-shell, black and mother-of-pearl. She poked at the sand with a feather, listened to the shouts of the children, sat up and counted them almost without thinking. Then she saw a huge wave rise up and watched paralysed for a split second as it reared above the kids. As she ran to their rescue it crashed down, but the kids were simply bowled over and washed up on the beach, swilling around in the soapy shallows, unharmed, not even scared. Behind her the mountains were blurred in haze. Cathy was still smoking. She too was looking out at the hills.

'They're beautiful in this light, aren't they?' Cath said.

'All iridescent. Lovely.'

They seemed to change colour. Violet, lilac, lapis lazuli, lavender, heliotrope, mauve. They changed as you approached in exactly the same way a face changed as it became familiar. That marriage changed. And love changed over the years. The mountains were unreal at this distance and to Jean that afternoon Rick and their marriage seemed unreal, insubstantial because of their temporary separation.

We cry in our own dark, she thought, make our own strange landfalls, but then how the devil did one make maps? Everyone was concerned with the same basic things and everyone seemed to make a mess of them as the years passed. Cath and Alberto, Rick and herself. It was the human condition. And suddenly she wanted Rick with her. The stirring of desire. She wanted to run her hand down his back, over his buttocks. Wanted to make him hard and feel him penetrate her flesh. The old biological urge. And it didn't matter that moment how many other women he'd screwed, nor how many men she'd had. The only enduring passion she'd felt was for Rick. It had survived all the quarrels and betrayals. It was the only thing that mattered. That strength at core. And their mutual love for the children. If she left Rick, what guarantee was there that she'd find another man who suited her better, who didn't bore her and who never even glanced at another girl's bottom and never did an irresponsible thing or acted stupidly on the impulse of the moment? There was no such guarantee. In this life you could count on nothing.

She remembered the first time Rick had been unfaithful. About three years after they were married. It had hurt her badly. And she couldn't understand it though he had tried to explain. She now supposed he hadn't been able to understand it either. He too was in the dark. Instead of simply saying: she turned me on, I wanted to fuck her, I did, he'd kept insisting that it meant nothing. She understood now. It was curiosity, exuberance, the shape of another body, the excitement of novelty. Any and all of those things. And more. But she'd taken it as an act of supreme disloyalty. A deliberate attempt to destroy the love they shared. In revenge she'd made love to a friend of Rick's at a party, almost in front of him. Rubbing his nose in it. Revenge and defiance. During the next few months she'd made love to several men. but that had turned sour. She'd used men to get her own back on Rick, not because she'd really wanted them. Neither had she really enjoyed it for her motive had not been pleasure, but to hurt Rick for the hurt he'd done her. It was interesting to find out about other men, but it didn't alter the fact that it was only Rick she really wanted.

Yet she had succeeded in hurting him. At that party he'd been cool and detached, but afterwards smashed his fist through a window, cutting his knuckles to the bone. It was what he'd wanted to do to her really, she supposed. And the following day, a Sunday, they'd stayed in bed, asking each other's forgiveness, swearing undying love, believing that their experiences had brought them closer. And so they had in a way. Rick was more attentive, more passionate than before. She had returned to him enriched as it were, but there was a shadow in their relationship, a sadness. And perhaps deep down Rick felt a resentment, an insecurity, that she could never erase. Certainly he'd had other women since. On the other hand she had felt such guilt, not for making love to someone else, but doing it for the wrong reason, that she'd jumped off that merry-go-round of tit for tat. It was no good. It didn't work for her. Brief affairs on a purely physical basis didn't do anything for her. They might for Rick, but not her. She wanted far more. Her expectations were far higher. Despite his faults Rick was better than one-night stands with men who had little else to offer her. Anyway she was only really turned on when her emotions were involved.

Now if some man were to come along with whom she could fall deeply in love . . . But that was a dream, a fantasy. And while she was living with Rick it would never happen. It took time and she was too involved looking after the children to go out looking for love that might turn out to be a myth anyway. For who was to know that the pattern would not be duplicated? Three years and the same thing all over again. It was not fair. But she'd learned to accept ages ago that life had little to do with what was fair or not.

'Cath,' she said. 'Have you ever considered how unfair it is to be a woman?'

'Constantly. I've known it all my life.' Cath laughed. 'But there's nothing much we can do about it unless we transfer our wombs to the men.'

'On the other hand,' Jean said. 'I suppose men believe that the odds are stacked against them too. I once heard Rick say it was easy for a woman. If she's halfway attractive, she can get laid, if that's what she wants, any time she likes. A man can't, not that easily, no matter how attractive.'

'Yes, but he misses the point. It's not just a question of getting laid,' Cath said. 'At least not usually.'

'Perhaps it is for a man.'

'And perhaps it is for a woman when all's said and done.'

'Oh I don't know,' Jean said. 'Let's get stoned tonight when we've put the kids to bed.'

'Lovely idea.'

Hair bleached from the sun, stiff and tangled from the salt, bodies bronzed and tingling, they drove up the sandy hill to the highway. The islands were black now with the sun setting, the sea an orange shimmer. A few dusty palms were silhouetted against the geometric hills. They drove towards Lima, the children chatting away in the back, and joined the freeway, flyovers spanning the road, shanties like beehives in the hills, buzzards still scavenging and the city in front smouldering with a reddish glow. Jean felt regenerated by the sea and sun. It was good to be in such a place, she felt, and light-years from those bleak tenements where she'd spent her first eighteen years. Her marriage might not be perfect (whose was?) but it was basically all right. And she was the mother of three children she adored. Sadness, regret, nostalgia were spectres to exorcise. Even if that took a little alcohol.

Alberto and Rick drove the eight-hundred miles to Guayaquil in two days. Alberto drove the first morning, the desert a kaleidoscope of mineral colours, the sea sparkling in sunlight. At Chimbote, a natural bay hemmed in by jagged cliffs, they stayed for a late lunch. It was a dirty town, a mass of shanties tapering down to the fishmeal factories, the smell pungent. Rick drove through the afternoon to Trujillo, mountains a grey ascetic backcloth. They stopped for a drink at a bar overlooking the plaza with its wooden balconies, then continued past the ancient ruins of Chan Chan north to Chiclayo. There they stayed the night, got drunk on the local beer and swam their hangovers away at a beach in the morning. Alberto talked the whole journey. He related anecdotes about his army experience and his childhood in Havana, Rio and Washington.

'My father was in the diplomatic service, that's why we moved around so much,' he explained. 'We had a great time, but I didn't really appreciate it then.'

'What was Havana like, pre-Castro?'

'They say it was decadent and wild, but I was too young. I just remember the sailing and fishing. I enjoyed Rio the most. I was fifteen and had a ball. I'd always got plenty of cash and it was teeming with whores. We used to take them to the beach at Ipanema and have barbecues at night.'

'I didn't know what it was like to have money until I was about thirty,' Rick said. 'Those first three years in Lima. It was the War until I was nine or ten. Rationing. We lived on stewed rabbit, dried eggs, corned beef and dehydrated potatoes, but I wasn't really aware of the shortage. I remember my Dad building a shelter in the sandpit at the top of the garden, barrage-balloons like trunkless and legless elephants, smokescreen tubs and black-out curtains . . .'

'It never touched me at all in Havana,' Alberto said.

'It was worse in the 'fifties,' Rick said. 'After National Service I worked in all sorts of jobs for peanuts. Even as a motor-roller driver for an asphalting firm I never earned more than twenty quid a week. Once I worked in a brewery as a clerk for five. That didn't last long. I got the sack. You see they gave us all two pints a day, but I was in an office with three girls who didn't touch the stuff so this bloke and me used to split their share . . . Even when I first started teaching I was only picking up about forty a month. It was the austerity drove me to South America.'

'In search of the good life?' Alberto said grinning.

'Something like that. I could never afford a car in England then. We went everywhere by trams that rattled and clanged over cobbled streets, past blue-slate walls blacked by soot and grime, gasworks and canals. Every so often you'd get a whiff of carbon monoxide or tar or coal-gas . . . I couldn't stand that city.'

'You and Jean both come from Birmingham, don't you?'

'Yes, right, but we've both always itched to get away . . . Incidentally, I meant to ask you, how's it going with Cathy at the moment?'

'Man, she's driving me crazy,' Alberto said. 'Always on about money and responsibility. Nag, nag, nag. Sometimes I feel just like walking straight out. She's been talking about separation and divorce. Fine, that's fine with me, but it's the kids. She'd take the kids.'

'Women are all the same,' Rick said. 'They fall for you because you're the way you are, then they want to change you. Want you to fit their ideal of what a husband should be. And if you did change and become the way they wanted, they wouldn't find you attractive anymore. They'd fall for the first blue-jeaned guitar-toting, nomadic, longhaired and shiftless minstrel that came along. For a replica of what you yourself had been before you changed.'

'I can do without women, man. I mean without living with one.'

'I can't,' Rick said. 'I'm just being flippant.'

'You know the most exciting thing I've ever experienced?'

'You mean apart from sex? No, what?'

'Apart from sex or drugs, the most fantastic kick I've had is jumping from a plane, the tremendous speed before the chute opens, then that floating sensation as you come down, the ground coming up towards you. That's the greatest, man. That and actually flying. I'll have to take you up.'

'What about facing a bull?'

'Exciting, but terrifying. I've only worked with a bull at a *tienta* – that's a kind of trial. With cows usually. They can be fierce though. Would you like to try it?'

'Sure.'

'The other thing I like is a good scrap,' Alberto said. 'When I win, I mean. That's a turn on. I mean it actually makes me feel horny afterwards.'

By late afternoon they had crossed the Sechura desert and were approaching Tumbes, the scenery becoming tropical – scrub jungle, sugar-cane and banana plantations. They crossed the frontier into Ecuador with no more than a cursory nod from the green-uniformed soldiers who lazily cradled their automatic weapons, then hit the road to Guayaquil.

'Hope it's as easy on the way back,' Alberto said. 'I wish they'd searched us then. It would have been a lucky omen.'

There were blue mountains in the distance and beyond, the gleam of snowcapped peaks. Chimborazo, Rick thought. Along the shores of the estuary were small settlements of stilted huts and the occasional mangrove swamp. The brown water was sluggish, driftwood moving out to sea, some skiffs with lateen sails hugging the bank. When they stopped at a shack dominated by a huge Coca Cola advert, Rick noticed some big velvet-green-and-black butterflies hovering round their table. There was something alien and exotic about the tropics that appealed to him. He could imagine himself acting the part of some beat-up character in a Somerset Maugham short story.

'Like a green witch,' he said, 'the jungle holds me in its spell.'

'Wait, wait till we get to the city,' Alberto said laughing. 'All this green shit, man, it's where the grass grows, but I like cities and hotels and bars, not the wilderness.'

Guayaquil lay on an inlet of the river. Alberto drove towards the

Paradise of Exiles

hill close to its centre. It was a mass of rickety houses and rambling streets. From the top they could look out upon silver tongues of water, jungle sloping to the river's edge, and in the distance, snow on the mountains, remote and unreal. They booked in at a small hotel, showered and went out. Alberto seemed to know exactly where he was going. He led them into a small seedy bar and invited them through to a private room at the back. There followed an interminable wrangle in Spanish until finally the transaction was settled. Alberto handed over what looked to Rick like several fifty-dollar notes. In return he was given a brown-paper parcel. It was the size of a small suitcase. They left and walked back to the hotel. Albert undid the parcel. It was full of pale green dry grass, seeds spilling everywhere. Rick had never seen so much marijuana.

'Cheap, Rick. cheap! Now what we've got to do is split it up in our cases. Fill your socks and trouser-pockets, tuck it into your shirts, then repack so that at a glance you can't see a single stem or stalk, OK?'

It took them about half-an-hour.

'Now we'll just shove them under the beds, leave them and forget their existence.'

'Isn't that a risk?'

'Yeh, the whole trip is, but no one will be in to clean these rooms till tomorrow morning. We'll be off at the crack of dawn. Now let's hit the town.'

They ended up in a brothel on the fourth floor of a block of flats. It was an expensive place, red carpeted with red and black wallpaper, divans and chairs in red leather in each of the little bars and alcoves into which it was divided. There were half-a-dozen girls, *mestiza* and *mulata*, young and attractive, who moved about with a decorum that was intended, Rick supposed, to fit the decor. Alberto ordered whiskies. A couple of girls came over and politely enquired if they wanted company. Alberto bought them rum-and-cokes. He gave Rick a joint which he'd rolled at the hotel and invited the girls to smoke. Smiling, they refused. It was potent stuff. Within minutes Rick was feeling euphoric. He wanted to talk and struck off at a conversational tangent. Alberto listened, chuckling to himself and every few minutes remarking that it was great grass. That he felt really *high*, really floating.

55

David Tipton

'I was telling you about the War,' Rick was saying. 'Well, it was a good time for kids. In England anyway. The reality only hit us later. Patriotism was morally justifiable then. We believed we'd fought the right cause. Against fascism. Or our parents had anyway. It was only afterwards that disillusion set in. In a sense we nullified one evil with another – the atom bomb . . . Are you bored?'

'No, Rick, I like to hear you talk. I'm digging it. Groovy stuff, this grass.'

'The girls look bored.'

'They'll be happy with another drink or two.'

'Well, as I was saying, things are never so simple as they seem, never so cut and dry. It was a drab world, post-War. All those little colonial struggles that followed. Malaya, Kenya, Cyprus. And I was at grammar school. Discipline the touchstone. Allied with a kind of muscular Christianity. *Onward Christian soldiers, marching as to war,*' Rick sang the first two lines of the hymn. 'That was the spirit. Ironically, we also sang Blake's *Jerusalem*. All those hymns and, of course, the ritual beating of boys who infringed their fucking rules. I used to have this fantasy of crouching up in the catwalk during Speech Day and mowing the hypocrites and humbugs down with a bren. Just like Malcolm McDowell. All those inflexible instructors. Canons who caned, bishops who were buddies with brigadiers. It bred violence.'

'Sounds a bit like the place I went to in Washington. That was based on the traditional English school.'

'Fatal. I mean, look at us. Here we are in a brothel in Guayaquil with these delectable girls about to smuggle pot into Peru. How the hell did we end up here? We were violated by anti-life morality . . . You weren't so badly off with those girls from Ipanema, but me, man, believe it or not, I didn't even know what had happened when I had my first wet dream. The only sex instruction I got was stuff about rabbits and frogs and then some religious education bloke informing us an erection was a manifestation of shameful thoughts. Imagine! At the sweet and tender age of fourteen being told that. Jesus wept, man. For us. He must have done.'

'Wow, you're floating, baby. You're high.'

'Sure, sure . . . Listen, there was this Canon, Blount or Hunt, that was his name, or something like it. Said, believe me it's true, that syphilis was God's way of keeping people on the straight and narrow. Keep off the grass – it's a sign all over England's green and pleasant land. Keep off the primrose path of dalliance else you'll end up with the clap. Divine retribution. I was head in the clouds with Lawrence by then and could reject all that crap. But it took its toll. Some of those guilts probably remain. In the Army they showed us films about the horrors of the pox. One about some poor bloke in India, Empire period, who goes off with a *native* girl. Miscegenation. Copulation with the indigene. He gets the syph, of course. Close-up of his chancred cock. Bloke's married too. Has to tell his wife. Finally after harrowing scenes, poor bloke practically destroyed by shame and guilt is cured. Vows to be virtuous for ever and ever, amen . . . Pre-penicillin that film.'

Alberto was doubled up with laughter. The two girls who didn't understand a word kept asking him if Rick was an actor.

'No, he's a pop-star,' Alberto said. 'Used to play alongside the Beatles. Or was it with Mick Jagger?'

'Man, I was a bit before their time,' Rick said. 'Though I don't feel like it, I'm a survivor, sold my soul to the devil. Which reminds me of another Canon. At college. Got us to write an interpretation of Genesis. Religion rearing its ugly head. Well, you know it's all about fertility and the continuation of the species – Jewish variety. So I wrote this Jungian stuff. He flipped, that Canon. Sent me down for a month to mend my atheist ways. But change was in the air. I used to wear black suede shoes and a maroon velvet jacket. Revolt was spreading and acquiring a style through pop-music.'

'You mean Elvis and Little Richard? Great stuff.'

'Right,' Rick said. 'I saw this film, Jean and I saw it, *Blackboard Jungle*, Bill Hayley's *Rock around the Clock*. And my hero then was James Dean, stuttering and stammering and crazy-mixed-up like in *East of Eden*. Then I got hold of Kerouac's *On the Road*. Hit me for six, to use a cricketing metaphor. Right over the boundary . . .'

'Rick, Rick,' Alberto said, interrupting his drug-inspired monologue. 'We're up early in the morning. Let's go with these girls, then get back to the hotel.'

'No, I don't feel like a woman tonight.'

'You what? Come on, man, you've been talking a blue streak and kept them waiting. Don't worry about the money, I'll pay.'

'No, Alberto, you don't understand, I don't feel like it tonight. Besides, I've changed, I . . .'

'I don't believe it. Look, it's anonymous, no one will ever know. Don't you fancy them? You choose. Take your pick.'

Rick laughed. 'I'm a hypocrite,' he said. 'I just talk too much. Yes, I like Graciela, the slimmer one. Of course, I fancy them. My willpower's like jelly, if you want to know the truth. Come on, Graciela, *yo te quiero*. You're beautiful, *muy hermosa*.'

Smiling, Graciela took Rick's hand and led him down a narrow corridor. There were doors at intervals. She unlocked one and went in. It was small and dark with a red glow from the bedside lamp.

'Do you like my room?' she asked in Spanish.

'Yeh, it's *muy lindo*.'

Rick undressed and sprawled out on the bed. He noticed how white he was where his swimming-briefs covered him. The rest of his body was bronzed in the dim light, almost as dark as Graciela's. She began to take off her clothes as if performing a professional striptease. It was so artificial, so much an act that it didn't seem erotic at all. In fact Rick, high on grass, found it amusing. He began to laugh.

'Why you laughing?'

'*Lo siento*, Graciela. It's just that I feel good. We've been smoking marijuana.'

'*Yo lo sé*.' She smiled, lay down beside him and kissed him. Touching her, her smooth brown skin, didn't arouse Rick. He just felt relaxed.

'What's the matter?' Graciela asked.

'Nothing. I feel fine.'

Something about his failure to get a hard-on seemed to amuse her. 'I like you,' she said. 'You're different.' But she was also the more determined to please him. She moved down and began sucking him. She did it with expertise. Rick was hard within seconds, but enjoying it so much he didn't want to penetrate. He felt passive, oddly serene despite the excitement which was localised, distant, happening only to his penis. He watched her head moving, her long black hair draped over his belly. And he came quickly, almost involuntarily. Afterwards they shared a cigarette.

'*Mañana*, you return to Lima?'

'Yes.'

'*Que lástima*. Next time you come to Guayaquil, you come and see me.'

'*Por supuesto*.'

'Promise.'

'*Sí*, I promise.'

Not long afterwards he dressed, met Alberto and they went back to the hotel. The cases were as they had left them. That night Rick slept restlessly, strange dreams floating through his mind. Images of desert, jungle, the dark red shadows of the brothel, and the sea. In technicolour. Marijuana dreams. But in the morning he awoke clearheaded, no hangover, nothing. Alberto paid the bill while Rick packed the suitcases into the car. He was tense and nervous as Rick drove back towards the frontier.

'Now, Rick,' he said at one point. 'The moment of truth, the real kick. It's the risk that counts.'

At the frontier two Peruvian soldiers checked their passports, had a cursory glance round the car, then asked to have a look at their luggage. Rick went weak. His hands and knees trembled. Had he been called outside he didn't think he could have actually stood on his feet. He lit a cigarette. Thought incongruously that fear of cancer disappeared completely in such circumstances. Alberto was chatting away in eloquent Spanish. In the mirror Rick watched him open the boot. He heard one or two stray words. Questions. He didn't care to listen too carefully. Then Alberto was back. He smiled at the soldier, shook hands formally, cracked some mild joke.

'OK, let's go,' he said to Rick. Rick turned on the ignition, put the car into gear, and such were his nerves came off the clutch so fast the engine stalled.

'Steady. Take it easy,' Alberto said. '*Mi amigo no puede conducir bien*,' he said to the grinning soldiers.

Rick started again, slipped smoothly into second, then third, crossed

59

over into Peru, changed to top and built up speed to 100 KPH. Irrationally he expected to be followed. He wanted to put distance between them and the frontier-post. He scarcely noticed the blue of the sea to his right, a few stunted palms, the greenery gradually changing to the lunar landscape of the desert. Brown hills looming ahead like old copper coins. It was ten minutes before either of them spoke.

'My heart was in my mouth,' Alberto said. 'I had to open the top case. I thought they might even sniff the grass, but they hardly looked. Didn't even touch inside. I'd got all my dirty underpants and socks on top. As I shook hands I slipped them a couple of hundred *soles*. Just for the goodwill.'

'I thought I was going to shit myself.'

'Let's stop, smoke a joint and have a swim if we find a good spot. Relax a bit. We'll have a smash the way you're driving.'

Half-an-hour later they pulled up, had a dip in the sea to wash the sweat and dust away, smoked and lay back sunbathing.

'One thousand dollars-worth of grass in that car, Rick. It'll be three hundred for you at least.'

'Great. Thanks, man.'

'Let's get back to Lima fast. I've got to sell the stuff. Except for what we'll keep.'

They drove all day through the desert in four-hours shifts and continued during the night. Early the following morning they were back in the city. Within the week Alberto had brought Rick his three-hundred dollars. Things were looking up. Cathy had sold some translations to an American magazine. Rick sold some to a couple of journals in England. The financial situation was easing. He obtained a series of lectures for March at the British Institute. On the Romantics. It was wide open this country, he thought, as Alberto had said. Now they had enough money to buy a few luxuries. It was a good life, he kept telling himself, provided you snapped up the opportunities as they arose.

Chapter Five

Coming back from the printers Cath was held up for an hour in heavy traffic. Cavalcades of cars were moving slowly down Avenida Arequipa, some draped in red-and-white flags, others sporting slogans such as *El Perú Campeón Mundiál* in white paint. Peru had just beaten Argentina in an eliminator for the World Cup.

The convoy of their celebrating supporters honked their horns in unison and passengers chanted the names of the forwards who had scored the goals: Cubillas, Sótil. Others set off firecrackers. Cath's frustration began to turn to anger as she moved at a snail's pace in first gear, waiting for a suitable sidestreet to duck into. Already tired, she was in a hurry to get the children off to bed before Robert Redman's party.

No wonder the generals were pleased, she thought. Football victories were being treated with the jubilation usually associated with a military triumph. Neither the revolution itself, nor the subsequent propaganda had provoked anything like this enthusiasm. She lit a cigarette, then managed to nip into a narrow street that branched off to the right. When she arrived back at the flat, the sound of rhythmic klaxons still blared in the distance.

An hour later Cath had fed the kids and supervised their showers. They were in their bedroom watching TV. Alberto was ready to leave. He had shaved and dressed while Cathy was tidying up.

'Shall I see you there then?' he said.

'Yes, I want to finish some work and make sure the kids are asleep before I leave.'

'But you're definitely coming?'

'Yes, Carlos Henson is reading, and I want to take some copies of *Ayllu* round. I've got to ask Rick something too.'

'What?'

'Just something about the translations.'

Alberto left. Cath heard the front-door slam and the VW start up. She smiled. Robert's place was only a few blocks away, but Alberto had taken the car automatically. Perhaps he wasn't going straight there. She poured herself a shot of *pisco*, then went into her daughters' room. They were both in bed, reading. Her son who was only eight was already fast asleep. She kissed them all and told Anna, the oldest, to make sure they were good. Then she took her drink into the study.

Copies of the magazine were piled up alongside the bookcase. Cath counted out thirty. She wanted to give some to the Peruvian writers who would be at the party and perhaps sell a few others. She glanced at the cover again. A black-and-white photo of Nazca pottery that Julio Scorza had given her, the title superimposed upon it in yellow print. Very elegant. And the contents were exciting too. An article by Charles Olson on projective verse translated into Spanish, some English poetry Rick had collected, reviews, and a special section in yellow paper of Julio's recent poems in translation. She felt proud of this fifth number.

She put the copies in her briefcase, finished her drink, then left. Walking along the quiet jacaranda-lined street she caught a strong whiff of the ocean on the breeze, but her thoughts were still on the magazine. By now she and Rick had done so many translations they ought to get a collection together and try some publisher. It would make an interesting anthology and she saw no reason why it shouldn't be accepted. Such a book would certainly help her obtain a university post if she left Peru. She knew that Alberto would never leave. It was too easy for him to make a living in Lima. It was still an easy-going country – if you came from the middle-class. Alberto always had his family to lean upon if things got tough. They would always bail him out. But she found it demoralising to depend so much upon them. More and more frequently she toyed with the idea of leaving. Alberto was at home in Lima. Its bland good-humoured decadence seemed to suit him, but it no longer appealed to her. The trouble was that his family would surely try to stop her taking the kids. A woman needed her husband's consent to do so. That was the snag.

Arriving at Robert's she found that she was the first guest there. Sheila gave her a drink and she gave Robert a copy of *Ayllu*.

'Very impressive,' he said. 'I'll give it a plug in the *Herald*. Is Alberto coming?'

'I thought he'd be here by now, but you know him. He'll probably turn up later.'

'Come and have something to eat,' Sheila said. 'It'll soon go when the others arrive.'

Cath followed Sheila into the kitchen smiling to herself. While she and Alberto were on the verge of splitting up, here was Sheila obviously ready to merge herself in Robert's life, sacrifice her independence. Cathy could still remember the temptation to do precisely that and that special sense of invulnerability that she herself had so much enjoyed for a brief period once. That sensual cocoon. She could remember it all right, but didn't envy Sheila, not one iota. How long would it be before Sheila rebelled against the constraints and dependence that at the moment she seemed to accept so willingly and probably wouldn't acknowledge even if Cath were to mention them. It was odd. All recently-paired couples gave off this aura of innocence. You wanted to warn them, but that would have required an impertinence she lacked. Or was it simply an innate certainty that they would dismiss her warnings with the same complacency she had shown a few years before? There were things couples had to find out for themselves. But did one ever learn? She had seen the same blind optimism in people who had experienced several disastrous relationships. Perhaps she was becoming cynical, but the truth was she didn't really enjoy the company of couples at this stage of mutual identification. It was too exclusive. A walled-in defence, an Avila of the emotions. On their own Robert and Sheila were stimulating. Together they bored her. She preferred Rick and Jean who had lost that incestuous quality years ago.

When Rick and Jean arrived the party was in full swing. Robert's two large rooms were crowded, the guests spilling out onto the balcony overlooking the street. *Can't get no satisfaction*, sang the Rolling Stones. Several couples were dancing. Rick stood just inside the room looking the scene over. He'd had a few beers already, but was still sober. He caught sight of Robert talking volubly, moving around, smiling, black beard bobbing.

'Hi, glad you made it,' Sheila said.

'Hello,' Rick said. 'Have you seen Alberto?'

'Sure, he and Cathy are around somewhere. I heard that you two had a good time up in Ecuador.'

'Successful.'

'Don't know what they got up to,' Jean said. 'All I know is that Rick's been in a good mood ever since.'

'Come and tell me about the trip,' Sheila said.

'I'll go and find Cath,' Jean said and moved off. She wandered round the apartment. It certainly expressed Robert's flamboyant personality. There were collages of nudes cut from *Playboy* alongside Indian rugs, crossed spears and bows-and-arrows from the jungle. Books on the shelves were alphabetically arranged. A stuffed iguana was perched on his desk next to the typewriter. In the other room his bed with the emerald sheets was barred by shadows thrown from the red-and-green flashing lamp.

'Jean, you're looking beautiful as ever,' Robert said, coming across to her. 'When are you going to come round and see me at the office? We could have a drink together.'

'I'm not, not now you're living with Sheila anyway,' Jean said. 'I've told you that whatever happened between us was a long time ago. I had my reasons and it was nice, but I'm not going to repeat the experience.'

'OK, OK,' he said laughing. 'I was only joking. You still look lovely though. I can say that, can't I? Sometimes I can't imagine you're the mother of three beautiful babies.'

'Neither can I' Jean said. 'Except when I'm at home looking after them.'

Robert grinned, excused himself and moved away. Jean stood glancing at the books on one of the shelves. It had been an aberration, that incident with Robert. Something she'd never told Rick for it had happened while he was in hospital with hepatitis. She'd been alone and miserable. Robert had called round most evenings to see her and one night he took her to the cinema. When they got back he came in for a drink. One became several. She couldn't remember precisely how they'd switched from a conversation about the film to making love, but when he'd touched her she'd realised how much she needed to be made love to. It had been a conscious physical ache. She actually led him to the bedroom. Not expecting such immediate compliance he was nervous at first and consequently gentle. Afterwards he had felt guilty and wanted to leave. She had to exorcise his guilt. Explain that Rick had affairs, as he knew, so that he was not to feel disloyal on Rick's account. Robert said he felt guilty about 'using' Jean. She laughed at that.

'We all use each other,' she said. 'One way or another.'

The difficulty had been to persuade Robert that it was just a one-off affair. To explain without hurting his feelings. Men were so vain. They thought that once they'd made love to a woman she would want some sort of commitment. They couldn't understand, or some of them couldn't, that women could enjoy one-night stands, sex without love. That was their vanity. In the end Robert had seemed to accept it though he still felt obliged to remind her every so often; to suggest a repeat performance.

Oddly enough she had felt disloyal to Rick. He'd come out of hospital somewhat subdued and contrite, having decided to make certain changes in his way of life. Of course, he hadn't felt that way for long and Jean had only to remind herself of some of the hurtful things he'd done to her for any sense of disloyalty to evaporate. His periods of reformation didn't last and in a way she was glad. They tended to bore her. She'd been getting fed up with him since their return to Lima. The trip to Ecuador had done him good. He'd been more his old self. There was a paradox in that somewhere, she knew.

She sipped her drink and looked around for Rick. She found him in conversation with Sheila.

'You know,' Sheila was saying. 'I've heard so much about you and Jean from Robert. When I first met him he was always talking about you.'

'I'd no idea.'

'You really impressed him. He was always on about that trip the two of you made to the jungle.'

'When I swam a tributary of the Amazon, fighting off the pirhanas, and we got lost in virgin forest?'

'Yes, I think he tries to emulate you.'

'Everything gets exaggerated in the telling. You never know where autobiography ends and fiction begins.'

'Or vice-versa,' Jean said.

'Well, we had a few wild times together,' Rick said. 'But that's all in the past now.'

'Is it?' Jean said smiling. 'You've just been up to Ecuador with Alberto. Wasn't that a *wild* time?'

'What were you doing there?' Sheila asked. 'Everyone's wondering, or guessing, I should say.'

'They just went for the trip,' Jean said.

'People are saying you went to get some marijuana,' Sheila said. 'They all seem to know about Alberto anyway.'

'Marijuana!'

'It's just that I'd like to try some.'

'I can probably get hold of a bit,' Rick said.

'Haven't you got any on you?'

'I'll get you a joint if you want one,' Rick said smiling. 'Hold on a minute.'

'Don't run away.'

Rick left Sheila with Jean and went over to the balcony. Someone had changed the record. The Beatles were on. *Here comes the sun.* He found Robert outside talking to a short darkhaired woman and hovered round waiting to be introduced.

'I didn't see you standing there,' Robert said. 'We were just talking about you. This is Irma.'

'You're going to be my teacher,' Irma said.

'I am?'

'You're doing a series of lectures at the Institute this summer, aren't you?'

'On the Romantics, yes.'

Paradise of Exiles

'Well, I've enrolled in your class. I love English poetry and I want to know more about it.'

Irma, Rick judged, was in her late twenties. She had an intense, pretty face with high cheekbones, and an attractive figure. Slim-waisted, with small shoulders and breasts, but wide hips. In a navy-blue mini-skirt her thighs were brown and plump. She talked in animated fashion, her small hands gesturing constantly.

'You speak English very well,' he said.

'I use it at work all the time.'

'What do you do then?'

'I work at the airport. I used to be an air-hostess, but I don't fly any more because I've got two children to look after.'

'You're married then?'

'I *was* married. To a pilot. That's a cliché, isn't it? But we're separated now.'

'I'm sorry.'

'You don't need to be. I'm living with my mother and she helps with the children.'

'We've got three ourselves.'

'Robert told me you were married. Which is your wife?'

'The blonde lady over there,' Rick said. 'I'll introduce you.'

'She's pretty.'

'It's a strange institution, marriage,' Rick said. 'But then you obviously know all about that.'

'I was simply too young when I got married.'

'I think we're probably always too young. No one should get married until they're forty, I'd say.'

'How old were you then?' Irma said laughing.

'Too young. I'm still too young.'

At that moment Cathy came up, a look of eagerness on her face that Rick recognised. 'Rick,' she said. 'I'm so glad you could make it. The magazine's out. It looks really good.'

'Have you got a copy?'

'I'll get one.' A few seconds later she was back with a copy of *Ayllu*.

'Looks great,' he said. 'Have you sold any?' What does Julio think of it?'

67

'I think he was pleased though he pretended to be blasé, but after all he's got quite a splash. He wanted a dozen copies.'

'Did you give them to him?'

'I shall do, he'll publicise it for sure. Listen,' Cath said, 'I had an idea tonight and I'd like to talk to you about it. It occurred to me that we've got the basis for an anthology. I've got a whole bunch of rough drafts I did while you were in Guayaquil and I'd like to go over them with you. We want only the best translations for a book.'

Rick liked working with Cathy. She had energy, flair and awareness. He could have scarcely translated much without her intuitive grasp of ambiguities and her knowledge of the vernacular. More than anything else it was their work together which had decided him to accept his situation in Lima.

'Why don't you come round tomorrow evening and we'll make a start. Go through all the stuff we've already done.'

'Rick,' Irma said, 'I'll see you on the course then.' Rick introduced her to Cathy. 'Can I buy a copy of *Ayllu*?' Irma asked. 'Then I'll leave you two to talk.'

'Heh, don't go,' Rick said. 'You're not leaving yet, are you?'

'No, I'm going to have a dance.'

'I'll see you later,' Rick said. 'There's something I wanted to ask you. As a matter of fact I wondered if you'd like to come to the beach with us one of these days. We go a lot in the summer. Bring the kids.'

'That'd be lovely.'

'Are you on the phone?'

'I'll write the number down for you.' She went off to look for a pen, came back, handed him a slip of paper, smiled, and went away again. He watched her hips as she walked across the room, then turned back to Cathy.

'Is Alberto here?' Rick asked.

'I don't know whether he's arrived yet, but I know he wants to see you about something.'

'I'll go and look for him.'

He found him in the kitchen talking to a group of people about the recent Beatles' record. 'A musical parody,' he was saying. 'They take several groups and sing numbers in their respective styles. It's fantastic, man . . .' Alberto had been smoking dope. Rick tried to catch his eye. Without stopping the flow of his monologue, Alberto handed Rick a joint. Rick went off in search of Sheila.

'I'll see you in a minute,' he said.

After smoking the joint Rick found that the party became more in tune with his mood. Simon and Garfunkel were singing *Bridge over Troubled Waters*, Jean was engrossed in conversation with Robert and Sheila, and Irma, he noticed, was dancing with a tall elegantly-dressed Argentine businessman he vaguely knew. He saw Julio Scorza, hair raffish, a demonic expression on his face, moving suavely round the lounge in rhythm with his girl, Ana-Maria – the Inca princess as Robert had called her. And Cathy was deep in conversation with a Peruvian novelist whose obsessive and dogmatic Marxism Rick found boring.

It was good grass. Rick felt benevolently serene. He'd lost interest in conversation, or even in trying to impress Irma. Everything could wait and nothing worried him. Then Robert turned off the stereo and introduced the poet, Carlos Henson, who was going to read from his latest book. He waited for silence, then began, reading the lines with a slow, rhetorical cadence. To Rick the poems sounded portentous, if not pretentious, but he soon lost track of the Spanish.

When Carlos had finished several people made eulogistic speeches in praise of the book. Rick watched Julio Scorza who seemed to be smiling sardonically, then he began to laugh. Carlos Henson! How on earth did a Peruvian come to acquire such a name? He went over to congratulate Carlos Henson and Julio introduced him to a writer from the south who was quite drunk. He seemed absolutely certain that Rick was a CIA agent. Nothing Rick could say allayed his suspicions. He probably had the same paranoid attitude about all foreigners. In disgust Rick left him and began chatting to Ana-Maria. She was exquisitely beautiful, delicate, fragile, too exotic for his taste. He found Irma more sexually attractive. She had a sensuality that Ana-Maria lacked.

Robert had put on a record by the Beach Boys, and Julio took Ana-Maria off to dance. Rick wandered into the kitchen where he found Alberto on his own.

'I've drunk too much beer,' Rick said. 'It's spoilt the effect of the grass. Can't distinguish between the two now and my head's spinning.'

'I've got something that'll clear your head like magic,' Alberto said. He took a phial from his pocket and tipped some white powder onto the back of Rick's hand. 'Sniff this up,' he said. 'Take it like snuff. Look, I'll show you.' He sniffed carefully at the powder. 'Be careful not to blow it away.'

'What is it?'

'It's cocaine, man. In a few minutes you'll feel completely lucid.'

He was right. Within a short while Rick's mind did seem icily clear. He found that he was speaking Spanish better than he'd ever done before. Perfectly fluent. And he'd lost all traces of drunkenness.

'I've been looking everywhere for you,' Jean said, coming into the kitchen. 'Are you ready to leave yet?'

'It's still quite early.'

'Have a smoke?' Alberto said.

'I vowed not to take that stuff again,' Jean said. 'The last time it made me so high I had hallucinations, then I got an asthma attack. Rick had to force about six cups of black coffee down me before I recovered. I know it doesn't seem to have any bad effects on you two, but it does on me.'

'I'll drive you home,' Rick said.

'Are you fit to drive?'

'Alberto gave me some cocaine to sober up with.'

'By the way,' Jean said. 'Cathy's already left. She asked me to tell you not to be too late getting home.'

They said goodnight to Alberto, then left. Jean didn't know why she had begun to be irritated by the party, and felt guilty dragging Rick away.

'You needn't have left,' she said. 'Or at least you can go back if you want after you've dropped me at home.'

'No, I wanted to go too.'

'Did you fancy that girl with the fat bottom?'

'You mean Irma? She's married with two kids. I asked her if she wanted to come to the beach with us sometime. I think she's going to be on that course of lectures I'm giving at the Institute.'

'She's a bit highly-strung.' Jean said. 'I sensed a note of hysteria behind that coy manner of hers.'
'She seemed all right to me.'
'When it comes to women, Rick, you only see the surfaces.'
Rick wondered how transparent he was to Jean. He didn't even know she'd seen him talking to Irma. Yet she was aware as if by some extra-sensory perception that he'd met someone he fancied. It made him feel vaguely defiant. He didn't warn Jean about men she met at parties.
As they turned into the parking-lot beneath their block of flats she turned and kissed him. 'Do you know why I really wanted to leave?'
'I thought you were tired and worried about the kids.'
'No, I wanted to make love to you.'
He smiled. Acceptance was what nourished him. It was all so simple for him; he only really cared about the moment. He didn't seem able to relate the past to the present or consider how an action could affect the future. Perhaps the majority of men were the same. They followed the impulse and were blinded by it. But were women any different? Once she had expressed the desire her body began to respond even though her mind still harboured some resentment. Women were victims of their physiology too – though that meant wombs, a menstrual cycle. It made them more conscious of consequences, more in tune with the future. No, that was nonsense. They had simply been conditioned by a male-dominated society for centuries and it took strength to break out of the trap.

Back home Cathy checked that the children were asleep, poured herself a *pisco* and glanced through her folder of rough drafts. With hard work they would have a book ready in a couple of months and perhaps her friend, the American poet, Ashley Pullman, who had been in Lima three years before, could help find a publisher. She might even come to be regarded as an authority in the field, for as far as she was aware no one else was translating Peruvian poetry. Thus she begun to perceive an escape route in the success of their project.
She finished her drink, got undressed and into bed. She was glad she'd left the party. It had begun to deteriorate as the alcohol flowed. It would probably continue until dawn. Alberto would probably stay

until the bitter end, even disappear again for a day or two. Certainly he was well-stocked with marijuana. She wondered how long it would be before he was main-lining. Well, it was his life, his problem. She had stopped worrying about him. In the long run you couldn't prevent anyone doing what they wanted. She'd accepted that. Salvation lay within oneself. Nobody could help another to achieve it.

Julio walked briskly down Jiron Unión which was badly-lit at night. He'd been to see the old poet, Carlos Alcántara, in his rooms near the station. Julio admired Alcántara, but felt sorry for him too. Now unrecognised except by a few obscure critics, he'd once been the most highly-acclaimed poet of his generation. A bit of a dandy then, with a razor-sharp wit, he had written some beautiful sonnets, fine surrealist verse and an elegant eulogy to Machu Picchu and Inca civilisation. Now he was living in genteel poverty in a run-down pensión. In a sense he symbolised Lima itself, the city which preferred its writers dead or at least docile. In a subtle way it destroyed the best talents. If they chose to stay there and not seek voluntary exile abroad.

Julio reached Plaza San Martín, passing the cafés where there would be the usual gathering of journalists and painters who spent too much time in such places. The city created inertia and enervated talent. Though partly the fault lay with the artists themselves. After all, few societies actively encouraged creative talent. Why should they? No use arguing that a healthy culture was a gauge of a nation's vitality. Art was of little economic value. When Alcántara died he would be raised to the rank of 'great Peruvian,' an element in the city's heritage, but alive he was merely a scribbler who drank too much and had homosexual predilections into the bargain.

That evening, before he had downed too many *pisco* sours, his conversation was erudite, scintillating, though like the city itself he too was immersed in the past. When Alcántara first started to publish Lima had been a more glamorous place. At least for the educated and leisured class whose wealth was founded on the serfdom of the Indian. Fewer people were aware of the social injustices then and fewer still had felt guilty about them. It simply hadn't impinged upon their lives, not like it did now with shanty-towns surrounding the city, poets dying as guerrillas in the jungle, and a doctor from Buenos Aires leading a rebellion in Bolivia.

Ironically, Alcántara, a poet the city ignored, expressed a nostalgia that was peculiar to Lima. Often Julio had exhorted him to make poetry out of his experience in the bars round Rimac, which he still haunted, looking for young men who might be impressed by his reputation or in need of a good meal.

'Write about that,' Julio said. 'All of it. We want to know. I'd like to see your private journals, those written in the heart. Celebrate your homosexuality, it's nothing to conceal, not these days. No one cares any more. Dozens of writers have come out in the open.'

Alcántara had smiled. 'That's precisely it,' he said. 'My sexual tastes are my own business, no-one else's. I don't want to exhibit them in public. I want a purity in my poetry and in the language I use. I refuse to write confessional stuff to titillate the reader. It's beauty I seek in my work.'

They'd argued, but Alcántara was not convinced. Watching his face which was furrowed and deeply-grained, his eyes baggy and his shirt-sleeves frayed, Julio realised that Alcántara had given up the struggle. He watched him order another *pisco*, then knock it straight back.

'I leave all that to you young writers,' he'd said, smiling. 'Times might have changed, I don't know, but if you want it so much, you write your own confessional poetry.'

He would never change, Julio knew, for the acids of time, and disappointment, had eaten their way into his soul. His rebellious spirit had gone. He watched the once-handsome face, the iron-grey mop of hair over the collar of his jacket, the neat grey beard and the slack flesh of his neck. The gods had deserted him. As he crossed the plaza Julio wondered whether middle-age would leave him the same – defeated, impotent, out-of-fashion. It was a common enough situation and its possibility frightened him. He needed a drink himself, or the encouraging words of someone like Ana-Maria or Cathy Morales.

Jean took David's small chubby hand and strolled along the edge of the surf, her son toddling by her knee, bow-legged like a miniature

73

cowboy. It was a weekday and the beach deserted. Behind her Rick was swimming parallel to the shore accompanied by their daughters who had rubber-rings as supports.

Jean was glad to be on her own with David. She loved him with a sharpness that was special. His hair was bleached almost white by the sun, his eyes very round and blue, his body deeply suntanned. When she'd first known she was pregnant with David, by accident and so soon after Emma's birth, she had wanted an abortion. Recalling this she felt a pang of guilt and a fluttering sensation in her belly that was similar to fear.

There must have been a full moon the previous night, or a very high tide. The surf was embroidered by sea-wrack and debris. The ocean itself was rusty-coloured with flotsam and jetsam. As if some underwater cataclysm had fractured the sea-bed. A pungent odour drifted in on the breeze, not just the tang of salt, but mingling with it the smell of putrefaction, of rot. They stopped to examine the millions of dead snails, crabs, red and gravelly starfish, crustaceans and molluscs she hadn't even known existed, mother-of-pearl mussel-shells and those of purplish sea-urchins. Further along they found some dead fish and the carcass of a pelican. Pecking at titbits all along the tidal hem were dozens of marine birds.

Thinking she could hear the sound of distant gunshots she looked up suddenly towards the sandy hills, eroded and chancred by the centuries. Another disturbance in the city – there had been several since the revolution, though it had ceased to be an obsessive topic of conversation. Even Julio had scarcely mentioned it when she'd seen him at Robert's party. There had been no discernible changes in the country, but neither had she expected any. Now that their financial situation had eased they'd begun to enjoy the place just as they had done in the past. It was a good country in so many ways. She'd persuaded Rick to return and she didn't regret that. Here she wasn't tied to the home by children, nor harassed by domesticity for she had Isolina to help.

Jean had always been haunted by memories of the poverty and deprivation she'd experienced as a child. Unlike Rick she still felt that insecurity. Still thought of herself as poor. Rick might have given her a transfusion of his own confidence and opened up possibilities she wouldn't have had the temerity to envisage in the early days, but she never passed a beggar on the street without a vague sense of recognition. Passed his outstretched hand too quickly, afraid of his rotting nose or scarred legs, but more than that, afraid to look him in the eye. As if he could see through her and recognise something of her origins in her furtiveness. Underneath she felt conscious of a similar insecurity, the sullen shame, because having expected little from life she often asked for too much.

It was that background she had returned to Lima to avoid and despite revolution or occasional nostalgia she was glad to be there. She had more time to paint and write, more time to cook exotic dishes and, above all, more time to actually spend with the children, not just serving their essential needs, but watching them grow and develop.

Chapter Six

In March, the warmest month of the summer, Rick began his lectures on the Romantics. His class consisted of six women, including Irma. She was sitting at the front, smiling at him. An odour of expensive perfume pervaded the room. At first he felt a little nervous, confronted by such a sophisticated-looking group, dressed as they were in fashionable trouser-suits or mini-skirts and blouses, but gradually his confidence returned. Bored with marriage or dull part-time jobs for pin-money, beginning to feel their feet as feminist ideas infiltrated the Lima middle-class, his students were clearly receptive and likely to appreciate the Romantics.

After the lecture Irma waited behind for him. He took her for coffee in the library where she questioned him about some of the points raised in the classroom. Before she left Rick invited her to accompany him to the beach that afternoon. When he arrived home and told Jean she said: 'don't you think we could go on our own for once? We seem to have seen an awful lot of Irma over the summer.'

'About three times.'

'Well, it seems a lot, and if it's not Irma, it's Cathy, discussing poetry and translations all the time.'

'I thought such things interested you too.'

'You might think Irma's genuinely interested in poetry,' Jean said, 'But I don't. It's you she's really concerned about. When you talk about Shelley's ideas on free love or whatever, she thinks they must be yours. It's a cheap way of making women fall for you, using other people's poetry.'

'If I talk about poetry, I'm not doing it with an ulterior motive, at least I didn't think I was, though you make me wonder about it myself at times. I begin to feel guilty in advance.'

'It's just that I don't trust her, I don't know why. She's perceptive enough and quite capable of looking after herself so don't let her arouse your latent chivalry.'

'Of course not.'

They collected Irma and drove to the beach. Once there Rick went off for a swim alone, then walked along the sand with the children, leaving the two women sunbathing. When Irma tried to engage him in a discussion about the morning's lecture he was evasive and glad that Jean herself began to talk about Mary Wollstonecraft.

'She was one of the first feminists in a way, but even she was a victim of her emotions. She fell in love with someone who betrayed her, then tried to commit suicide.'

'Was that before she met Godwin?'

'Yes,' Jean said. 'You see it was all right for the men to have their far-out ideas, but the women had to face the practical responsibilities, and look what happened to them. Harriet, Shelley's first wife, drowned herself, and Mary, his second, became bitter and probably frigid after the death of her children. She was forced into irony. So much for Percy's platonic love, she said, when some Italian girl he'd idealised asked him for money.'

'Rick said that when they had to burn Shelley's body on the beach after he'd drowned in his yacht, Mary Godwin snatched his heart from the funeral pyre, and put it in a casket on her desk while she wrote Gothic thrillers.'

'Very symbolic,' Jean said.

'But from what Rick said this morning, I should imagine Byron was far more of a male chauvinist than Shelley.'

'It wasn't really his fault that women chased him all over the place,' Rick said. 'They wanted to possess him, not the other way round. I'm all for sexual equality, but often it seems that women don't really want it.'

'Crap!' Jean said.

'It's women who usually want one man exclusively.'

'You just don't understand,' Jean said. 'For a woman sex is usually an emotional experience.'

'I don't understand them, that's true, but I prefer their company to that of men – except for one or two close friends.'

'Ah, but you're much more discriminating in your choice of male friends,' Jean said.

'Here we go,' Rick said. 'Round in the same old circles. I think I'll go for another swim.'

'There you are,' Jean said. 'Typical. When the argument begins to go against him he takes refuge in some muscular activity.'

'I think I'll go for a dip too,' Irma said. 'Are you coming?'

'No, I'll keep an eye on the children.'

Rick plunged through the breakers, surfaced in cool placid water on the far side and swam out for two hundred yards. On his way back he caught sight of Irma moving through the water towards him. She turned when they met and swam back alongside him.

'Jean's right,' Irma said as they were strolling back to their place on the beach. 'Sex is an emotional thing for women.'

'Perhaps she's right, I don't know. How could I?'

When they dropped Irma off in Miraflores later that afternoon, Rick was surprised to hear Jean invite her for supper later.

'We're having a few friends round,' Jean said. 'If you'd care to join us.'

'I'd love to. I'll get my mother to babysit.'

It was a warm, humid evening. Until dinner Cathy, Julio Scorza and Rick went through some translations. Then, after they'd eaten the curry Jean had prepared, Alberto rolled some joints and offered them round. Sitting next to Irma on the divan, Rick was conscious of the immediate physical effect of the marijuana. It seemed to dull the intellect, but quicken the senses. Conversation flickered haphazardly from topic to topic. There were long pauses between comments. Voices seemed stilted and artificial though the jazz on the record-player sounded superb. And Rick's thigh which was pushed against Irma's tingled with the excitement of contact.

About midnight Jean said she felt tired and was going off to bed. It was a signal for the group to break up. Alberto wanted to go into town to find a bar still open, but Cathy was anxious to get home. They gave Julio and Ana-Maria a lift. Rick drove Irma back. He parked in the cul-de-sac near her house, turned to her and kissed her.

'I want to make love to you,' he said.
'Not now,' she said. 'There's nowhere to go.'
'We could go to the beach.'
'There isn't time. My mother will be waiting up. I'll see you after your next lecture.'
'That's ages.'
'Next Friday, but I must go now.' She smiled, kissed him briefly, opened the car door, got out. He watched her. At the front gate she looked back, waved. He started the VW and drove back cautiously because he felt so high.

When Rick climbed into bed and lit a last cigarette he disturbed Jean, but she said nothing, pretending to be asleep. She wanted the solitude of her own thoughts, the privacy of her insomnia. The ache in her left shoulder had come back. It frightened her. She was aware of some weakness in her lungs that she might have inherited from her father or even her grandmother. But to talk about it to Rick or anyone would have been a species of bad luck. As long as she didn't discuss her fears she could control and forget them more easily. Besides it was probably nothing, this nagging ache, and she didn't want to spend a fortune having tests and examinations at the clinic. If she were to tell Rick he'd go on at her until she went. If he himself had a pain everyone knew about it. Since he'd once had hepatitis he'd rush off to the clinic at the slightest discomfort, imagining cirrhosis, gallstones, an ulcer, kidney trouble, cancer or a weak heart. She preferred the uncertainty.

Rick was snoring mildly, so Jean eased herself out of bed, listened for a moment to the children's quiet breathing in the next room, then went into the kitchen. She made a coffee and lit a cigarette. Naked because the night was warm, her muscles aching, she decided to have a shower. With the door shut it would wake no one. She stood for a long time under the hot water, letting it steam and soothe away the fatigue she felt in her bones. She washed her hair. It was still golden, heavy and resplendent, but the three pregnancies had taken their toll of her body. Her breasts somehow seemed smaller. Certainly they sagged more while there was nothing she could do to restore the resilience of her belly. Instead of the firm convex curve she'd once had

David Tipton

there was a small protuberant pot of flaccid skin, still a bit wrinkled, which no matter how much she dieted wouldn't disappear. She could lose weight everywhere else. Off her boobs, her thighs, her bottom, but not her belly. No wonder Rick found younger women more desirable, she had lost her figure.

She resolved to exercise more for dieting alone was useless. Oddly enough Rick didn't complain about her figure, he never had done, but he grumbled when she went on a diet.

'I prefer you plump,' he'd so often said. 'A bit of flesh gives the body a springier feel.'

'It's not you I diet for,' she'd snapped back. 'It's for myself.' My own self-esteem, she thought now.

Rubbing herself down in the darkness, glancing out of the window at the lights of the city and the steely glint of the sea like a bruise between the high buildings, Jean noticed a face blurred by shadow, pressed against the window-pane in the flat opposite. It was their Italian neighbour, a dark-haired handsome man with a very pretty wife. Someone else who can't sleep, she mused, wondering what trivial quarrel or perhaps melodrama had kept him awake. Then she realised that he was looking at her – half-naked, the towel wrapped round her hips. His stare was disquietingly sexual. She smiled. It didn't displease her though beneath her amusement part of her mind was a little cynical. As she picked up her nightdress and padded away she caught a glimpse of his wife's shadow framed in the light of the door. Something about her posture made her certain that the couple had been quarrelling.

Rick had gone off to work when Jean got up the following morning and she didn't recall the incident until she saw the Italian's quite lovely wife by the wall round their little patio, cleaning out some boxes on the balcony. The woman waved and smiled. Jean waved back. An odour of spicy cooking and coffee wafted across. A few minutes later the wife was singing in Italian. Whatever had happened during the night had apparently been dissipated by the dawn. Or perhaps they'd patched over the quarrel by making love.

That afternoon Jean had to go shopping. When she returned to the apartment block the husband followed her into the lift. They ascended together. In careful, polite English he asked her questions about the children and commented upon the weather, but the whole time his eyes roved over her tight dress. Only when he got out did he look her in the face. Then she noticed that his eyes were yellowish and gleamed like those of a predatory tomcat. Afterwards she felt disturbed by the incident. In a way she was flattered. The implied compliment was good for he self-esteem. But in another sense she felt insulted, even assaulted. For him she was an object. He had summarised her desirability and marked her somewhere between A-minus and C-plus. In exactly the same way that Rick assessed other women

'She's got a sexy arse,' he would say. Or: 'I like the curve of her breasts,' picking out one or other of a woman's attributes as if she were a filly at a horserace. Most men were like that, Jean thought, dominating without being aware of it, patronising, too-self-assured and far too bloody egotistical. Sometimes she despised them all. Rick, Alberto, Robert, Julio and her nextdoor neighbour whose wife was so obviously devoted to him. *She* scarcely noticed Rick, for example, though Rick had certainly noticed her. Yet this sense she had that she knew more about men than they knew about women gave her a feeling of devious power. When Rick came home, to test his reaction, she told him about the incident. Predictably enough he laughed and came out with a clumsy compliment. She liked that, but also acknowledged that there were times when she wanted to live alone, dependent upon no man, in any way.

Making notes for his lecture, Rick became obsessed by a plan. Which was to write a long sprawling poem based on the years he'd spent in Lima. Or perhaps a novel. He started to jot down significant incidents, exciting details around which to build his work. Certain people he'd become involved with, and more recently, the trip to Ecuador and the revolution. Then he realised such a work would be a kind of lie, a gross distortion, for it would emphasise the adventure, the exotic at the expense of other tracts of living. Perhaps three-quarters of his time, two-thirds at least, was spent in much more mundane activities. He spent approximately one-thousand two-hundred hours per year teaching English in the college tucked away in the foothills on the edge of the city and about twice that amount of time sleeping. He scarcely wrote a word about either activity. Yet both were essential. For obvious reasons. He tended to concentrate in the notes on action. He forgot that three or four nights a week, perhaps two-hundred a year, Jean and he stayed at home, content to be there, listening to their records or reading. Between them they probably read two hundred books a year. A whole variety of literature. Anything that looked interesting in the Institute library or that Rick picked up in paperback from the American bookshops. There were the magazines that came from England and the books by Peruvians he read in order to translate. And there were the evenings they went to one or other of the air-conditioned cinemas. Often twice a week. Or to a restaurant, just the two of them, gossiping about friends, reminiscing, or being amusing and superficial. There were the hours he devoted to the children. At least a thousand a year.

It was time spent quietly in such ways that was the meat of his life and which gave it richness and texture, gave him much of his contentment. Yet when he made notes for a novel, an autobiography or a poem (was there any real difference for all three forms fictionalised reality in one way or another?) it was the relationships, the excitements he chose to write about. So the complexity, the woven fabric was oddly dislocated, even perhaps diminished. Still pondering this he drove down to the Institute for his Friday morning lecture.

In the library afterwards he was joined by Irma. She told him that the women in the group had asked the director to extend the course if Rick were prepared to continue as several of them were planning to study English Literature at university.

'Suits me,' Rick said. 'I could go on with the Romantics until the end of the year. Look, shall we go for that drive into the hills we planned the other night?'

'You know, Rick, there's just one thing that worries me.'

'What?'

'Jean.'

'Well, she's gone down to the beach with Cathy. I said I wanted to do some work and would join them later.'

'No, it's not that. I just think she knows about us, or has guessed. I don't want her or anyone to get hurt.'

'No one will get hurt,' Rick said. 'I just want you very much. I like you. I like being with you.'

'But you love Jean, don't you?'

'Of course, but let's not analyse anything. Let's just accept the moment. Don't let's start feeling guilty. That spoils everything.'

'I can't control my feelings as well as you can.'

They drove through the city, up the central highway for five miles, then into the motel. Invisible from the road, only the sign *Tu y Yo* indicated its whereabouts. They went up the circular drive and emerged among some white flat-roofed bungalows, each with its own garage. The sun was hot, the nearby hills pale ochre against blue sky. Bourgainvillaea climbed the adobe walls and dusty eucalyptus trees gave the place some shade. An Indian directed Rick's VW towards one of the chalets. He stopped in front of the garage and the doors swung upwards automatically. He moved inside. The doors shut. They were alone. They got out and went through an adjacent door into the bedroom. It was very clean and simply furnished. A bed occupied at least half the space. Round it were mirrors. Irma smiled and as if on an impulse checked the sheets. The phone rang. Rick picked it up.

'If you want anything,' a voice said, 'we'll send it up through the hatch. Please call for the bill before you leave. It's two-hundred *soles* for two hours.'

Rick smiled wryly. They were locked in, prisoners of desire. Very symbolic. Only one way out – through the garage which was locked from the outside. He went into the small bathroom. Toilet, bidet, shower. He switched on the light. It was red, but there was light enough in the room without it. He put his arms round Irma and kissed her.

'It's so anonymous,' he said. 'Just imagine, no one in the world knows where we are or could possibly guess. It's a strange feeling. As if we've disappeared and are invisible for two hours.'

'I'm not sure I like it. I've never been to one of these places before.'

'You haven't?'

'No, honestly, have you?'

'Once, a long time ago.'

83

'I feel a bit like a whore somehow. Can you understand that?'

'Yes, but it's silly. You're yourself. I'm myself. This place is just convenient. It's neutral and anonymous. That's all. Like a hotel room.'

He kissed her again. He sensed that he'd have to take it slowly, allow her to adjust to the room, the situation. For he could understand her feelings. The purpose of such a place was so blatant. It could as it were assault the sensitivity with its basic assertion – the mirrors, the bed, the functional bathroom. He began undressing her, undoing buttons, zips. Her hands were inside his shirt, caressing his back.

'I won't be a minute' Irma said, disengaging herself and going into the bathroom. Rick took off his shoes and socks. He lay back on the bed. 'Don't look,' Irma called. 'Please.'

'Why not?'

'I'm so fat. My bottom's too fat.'

'It's beautiful,' Rick said. 'It's your bottom I love.'

He heard her laugh and then she came out. She put her clothes on the chair and slipped under the sheet beside him. She was laughing quietly. Rick was very excited. The novelty. Her plump thighs, wide hips and round bottom. Billowy, big-curved, bouncy were the words that came into his head. And her slim shoulders, slim arms, small hands touching him lightly, delicately. His fingers slid from her thick pubic hair into the wetness of her cunt. Touching her clitoris he moved between her thighs, penetrated easily, his right hand beneath her bottom. The wet kisses, the warmth, the sticky juices, riding away like a twenty-year old. And the cry that came from him, almost a shout, caused Irma to say involuntarily, 'ssh, ssh!'

Rick slipped down, his head between her thighs, kissing her lightly, exploring the hard little kernel of clitoris, taking it between his lips, feather-flicking it with his tongue, one finger just inside her and the other a joint up her anus, wet with mucus and spittle. Fingers, mouth and tongue moving independently. And as he sensed her coming he increased the speed, the pressure, felt her clitoris erect, then get smaller. He almost lost it for a moment, but went on and she came convulsively. He felt the palpitations of her anus like a tight little muscle. Then she closed her legs, Rick moving away. He looked up. She smiled. Brown eyes soft and tender.

'That was lovely,' she said.

They talked for a while and smoked cigarettes. The hired room no longer seemed so alien, but almost pleasant. They examined each other's bodies from different angles in the wall mirrors and slowly began to make love again. This time it was at a lower voltage, familiar, sweat slippery between them. Rick took much longer to come so they switched positions, experimenting. Afterwards they showered together, then Rick phoned for the bill and sent the cash down the hatch. They left. The garage door was open and no one around. They got into the VW, backed out and drove towards the city in the middle of the afternoon, a cool breeze in the car. He dropped Irma in Miraflores.

'When shall I see you?' he said.

'I'll call by, or if not, next Friday at your lecture.'

Rick headed for the beach doing 100 KPH along the freeway and singing aloud. He drove down the dusty track to El Silencio, spotted Jean and Cathy at the far end. Emma and Sara greeted him like a long-lost wanderer. He hugged them both, kissed Jean, loving her very much as he always did after an *infidelity*, feeling free and totally himself, independent yet overflowing with warmth, gloriously alive. As if a weight had been lifted from his shoulders or from his mind. He took the children down to the sea, then went for a long swim alone, way out, tempting his luck, taking a bit of a risk, giving the activity an extra kick, for he knew about the sea, its power and at times, treachery. Enough anyway to treat it with respect.

He enjoyed the thrill of going a mile out though still encompassed by the long arm of the bay. Swimming back it crossed his mind that taking risks was an unconscious atonement, an offering to the gods, his way of placating fortune. He took risks because he was appalled by the thought that all this joy should ever end. The awful finality of it. And if you flirted with danger you showed your contempt for it. And one should never show fear. That was unlucky. Fear was the smell of stale blood, a carcass after a day in the sun, the stench of hospitals, of vomit, or rotten eggs. A sewer smell. And the bad breath of it could infect your life. Poison it. You had to eliminate fear. Snap your fingers at it. Impossible perhaps, but you could help to cancel it out by doing things that took some courage. It was surely the supreme virtue. To smile back at the sour grin of your own fear.

Cathy woke from a deep sleep with a vague sense of anxiety. At first she thought the alarm must have gone off and it was time to get up. She fumbled for a cigarette, becoming aware of the strident sounds of rock-music coming from the lounge, of Jagger's abrasive voice.

'Oh Christ!' she said. Alberto must have arrived home. She glanced at the clock. It was three forty-five. The stereo was turned up to full-volume. She got out of bed, brusquely putting on a dressing-gown. When she turned on the light she caught a glimpse of herself in the mirror. Her face looked gaunt, eyeshadow smudged, her hair tumbled about and straggly. Like a mop, she thought. Her eyes were bleary from lack of sleep. A spasm of self-disgust assailed her, whipping up her temper to boiling-point.

'Turn it off, you'll wake the whole goddamn neighbourhood,' she said bursting through the door, her voice rising to an almost hysterical pitch. Then she stopped. Alberto and four others – long-haired, dressed in jeans and Indian-style ponchos, were lounging around the floor, smiling inanely at her as she stood framed in the doorway. One of them was tapping out the rhythm with his foot, another eating from a saucepan of rice Cathy had saved from the evening meal. An acrid smell of marijuana pervaded the room and mingling with it the smell of frying fat.

'Come and have a smoke,' Alberto said. 'It's great stuff. We're all high.'

She looked at Alberto's bloodshot eyes, the weak smile, his face so completely relaxed it appeared almost amorphous. She ignored him and strode through to the kitchen. A dark-skinned girl was frying eggs on the stove. She smiled in an amicable but detached way and continued cooking. Cathy returned to the lounge and walked straight up to Alberto.

'Perhaps,' she said in a more controlled tone, 'you'll be so kind as to tell me what the fuck's going on.'

'Come and meet everyone.'

Paradise of Exiles

'I've no desire to meet anyone at four in the morning, especially a group of goddamn hippies spongeing on your hospitality. You're a fool, Alberto, a bloody fool.'

'Heh, baby, what's wrong?'

'Listen to the Stones, man,' one of the hippies said. 'Great sound.' Cath stalked over to the stereo and switched it off.

'I feel alien vibrations,' someone said and got up. As if this were a pre-arranged signal the others began to stir themselves, collecting their things, putting cigarettes in pockets. The girl came from the kitchen with a plate of fried eggs to eat with the rice.

'Oh you're going then,' she said, the detached smile fading slowly.

'Yeah, we're off. See you around, *hombre*,' one of them said to Alberto.

'Don't go yet,' Alberto said.

'Man, we don't want to get you into some heavy shit.' In a shambling phalanx they sauntered through the door. Cathy heard them going downstairs, then the bang as the front-door shut.

'What's wrong, honey?' Alberto said obtusely.

'You have the nerve to ask me that!' Cath said. 'I've been working hard all day except for a couple of hours at the beach, getting a meal for you, then translating tonight, and I haven't set eyes on you since this morning, I mean yesterday morning. I'm woken up at dawn by a bunch of your friends playing records and eating us out of house-and-home, and you ask me what's wrong! Alien vibrations, that bum had the arrogance to say.'

'Cathy, what's happened to you? I invited them back, we wanted you to join us. You can't just throw people out like that. What's happened to your famous American hospitality?'

'Alberto, this is the bloody limit. I'm fed to the teeth with your comings and goings, your drug acquaintances, your goddamn music. I'm through with it. This is just the last bloody straw. That's what's wrong.'

'What a bitch you can be at times!'

'I want a separation,' Cathy said. 'As from now. You can sleep here tonight and in the morning pack some stuff and move out.'

'Where to, for Christ's sake?'

87

'I don't much care. To your mother's or to one of your so-called friends. Anywhere.'

'Let's talk about it in the morning, OK?'

'We'll discuss the arrangements, yes. But I'm telling you, Alberto, we're through. *Finito*. I've taken all I intend to take. I want you out and I want a divorce and I want to go back to the USA. With the children.'

'You can't do that.'

'I can and will.'

'Come and have a beer and we'll talk about it.'

'There's nothing more to say. I'm tired and I want to get some sleep. I'm going back to bed.'

'Well, we'll talk in the morning.'

'Nothing's going to change my mind, I'm telling you. You can find a place of your own. You're hardly ever here anyway.' She noticed the plate of fried eggs congealing on the table, the half-finished saucepan of cold rice on the floor, the empty or half-empty bottles of beer, the ash and cigarette-butts, the greenish smell of marijuana. 'Jesus!' she said. 'What a mess!'

'Don't worry so much,' Alberto said. 'That's the trouble, you worry all the time.'

She threw Alberto a look of exasperation, walked through to the bedroom, lit a cigarette and lay down on the bed. Her head was thumping and grey light was filtering through the curtains. Angrily she nubbed out the cigarette and pulled the sheet over her head, her determination to keep to her decision filling her mind. A few minutes later she heard Alberto snoring on the divan in the lounge. But she couldn't sleep. In three hours she was due to lecture on English grammar and syntax to a group of engineers at the Catholic university. In two hours the children, if they weren't already awake, would be up, clamouring for breakfast, looking for their school-clothes, whining, squabbling, asking questions, laughing, joking, making their small but insistent demands. Cathy felt as if she were on the edge of a nervous breakdown. Something had to give. Some tension had to snap. Well, she was resolved not to revoke her decision. Alberto would have to find a place of his own. And that was simply that.

Twice more after his lectures Rick drove Irma to the motel. It was a little odd to switch from discussions on poetry to making love, or at least Irma seemed to find it difficult. It was easier for Rick. He didn't feel much sympathy with the ethereal nature of Shelley's love poems. He was more down to earth. And infatuated with Irma. For Rick the charge was sexual and the lectures merely accentuated the charge. On the other hand Irma took to calling round at his apartment when he had returned from college in the afternoon and Jean became increasingly cool towards her. In the end Rick suggested to Irma that they would have to meet somewhere else. He didn't want to flaunt their friendship. It was something private, between the two of them, he explained, and if Jean were hurt he would feel guilty. Guilt could infect, even ruin their relationship and he didn't want that to happen.

One afternoon when he arrived home from college Rick heard voices from the patio raised in argument. Jean and Irma.

'No one has ever spoken to me like that before,' he heard Irma saying.

'In which case it's about time,' Jean said. 'I'm simply telling you to stop chasing my husband.'

'But I'm not.'

'Don't tell me you come round here to see me.'

'I come to see you both.'

'Well, I'm fed up of seeing you round here every afternoon of the week and I'm tired of your long talks with Rick.'

'There's nothing to get jealous about.'

'Jealous of you! Don't be so presumptuous! I don't particularly like your company, but what you do, or for that matter, what Rick does at the Institute is no concern of mine. I just don't want you coming round here all the time.'

'Well, that's clear enough anyway,' Irma said. 'You're wrong though. There's nothing between Rick and myself. I like being with you as much as I like being with him.'

'The sentiment's not mutual, I'm afraid.'

'All right, I know where I'm not welcome.'

'I hope so.'

Rick hadn't heard Jean talk in such a way before. It had been like listening to a second-rate soap-opera. He was paralysed, unable to intervene. Irma emerged suddenly from the kitchen, brushed past him, smiled briefly and automatically, and let herself out.

'What's been going on?' Rick asked.

'I told Irma she's been coming round too often, that's all.'

'For Christ's sake!'

'For a change I'm putting myself first.'

'But . . .'

'Say what you like, Rick. You know very well I've never liked her much. And you know why.'

'Surely you're not jealous.'

'Call it what you like. That's the way I feel and I'm not going to start an argument with you about it. You can discuss Shelley with Irma at the Institute. If that's what you really want from her.'

'She's just a friend.'

'Don't say any more . . . Let's get the kids and go for a ride in the car. We can go to Chorrillos and you can have a swim while we watch them unload the fishing-boats.'

Rick said no more. They drove down to the quayside in silence.

They passed two large manta rays and a small blue shark. Sara and Emma stopped to have a closer look. About four-foot long, its bluish-purple skin wrinkled like velvet, the shark was rough to the touch. Rick tipped back its snout, then tried to prise open the jaws, but the glutinous mouth was shut tight. They dawdled on past piles of mackerel and bonito. The sky was leaden, the sea grey with a trace of rust, and mist was making visibility poor beyond the fishing-boats bobbing on the water. Rick looked at Emma with her copper hair and Sara who was chatting to Jean. They were beautiful, his daughters. They were more important to him than anything else. He lit a cigarette. His hands reeked of mucus from the maw of the dead shark. For a moment he watched some pelicans diving for fish nearby, then he looked back at the cliffs towards the headland, hazy in the mist. He felt tense, wound up like a spring.

'I'm going to dive in off the steps at the end of the jetty,' he said to Jean. 'I'll meet you back on the beach.'

'How long will it take you to swim in?'

'Only about twenty minutes.'

He stripped off his shirt and jeans, gave them to his wife, then plunged in. A gaggle of Indians jostled at the end of the pier, watching him. They smiled. They were highly amused. Rick was a crazy *gringo*, acting the part. Jean was embarrassed. She took her daughters' hands and walked away.

The shock of the fish-smelling water took Rick's breath away. He struck out through the swell, the taste of salt clean in his mouth. He felt that nothing could touch him. The sea was sanctuary from the labyrinth of emotion and thoughts in which he was frequently trapped. Even his guilt evaporated. No one was going to dominate him. Whatever he did he was answerable only to himself.

On the beach Jean was waiting for him with a towel. As he waded in from the shallow surf, the children jumped up and down, shouting to him.

'Come and get dry,' Jean said. 'You look blue.'

'Let's go out for dinner, tonight,' he said.

'Yes, why not?'

A few days later, coming home from college, Rick called in at Irma's. He saw her sitting on the low wall outside her mother's house. She was wearing a smoke-blue mini-skirt and with a pang he noticed the plump spread of her thighs against the pressure of the brick.

'Hello,' he said. 'I just came by to find out when and where we can meet.'

'Now that your wife has barred me from your apartment.'

'What did she say exactly?'

'Just told me to stop chasing you. She's right, Rick, you know, I was becoming involved, I couldn't help it. That's why I kept calling round. It was like an obsession. Well, Jean brought me to my senses.'

'Which means what?'

'That I don't want to go to that motel again. It's finished. I like you, but as a friend.'

'As a friend?'

'I like talking to you, but that's all I really want. I'll see you at the Institute when you do the rest of your lectures.'

'You mean it's over?'

'It's changed. The other day changed it. I'm sorry, that's the way I feel.'

'So am I. It had only just started.'

'We made a mistake.'

'You mean you don't want to make love anymore?'

'That's not the point.'

'It is.'

'Well, that's all over, yes.'

Rick got back into his VW and drove home through Miraflores. He had a coffee, then took Emma to the nearest beach. They clambered over the stone breakwater and crouched down looking across the slate sea, watching the rise and ripple of the waves. A mottled-olive fish flipped over in the surf. On the rocks were some starfish like red spiders.

Returning to the car Emma found a dying bird. Its beak was opening and closing feebly. Rick wondered whether he should kill it, but was unable to bring himself to do so. He held Emma's hand, consoling her, and together they sat on the wall, spray in their faces. He was beset by images of Irma and had a strong desire to bury his head between her thighs. Instead he kissed the top of Emma's red hair, whisked her onto his shoulders and walked back to the promenade.

'Poor bird,' Emma kept saying, almost in tears.

That weekend Jean suggested a picnic at the beach. She was hoping that it would snap Rick out of his depression. It irritated her for she was partly the cause of it, she supposed. Though starting to teach at the college again was another factor. As was the whole business of Alberto and Cathy. Far from showing sympathy for them Rick actually seemed a little envious of Alberto's apparent freedom, his quick switch to a bachelor life. Alberto was now installed in a bedsitter, able to come and go as he pleased, accountable to no one. The fact that he wasn't overjoyed about it didn't seem to occur to Rick. Not even when Cath said she had seen far more of Alberto since the separation.

'Let's go to Punta Hermosa,' Jean said. 'You've been brooding for days and it's enough to try the patience of a saint.'

'There's nothing wrong with me,' Rick said. 'It's you who's in some sort of mood.'

'That's absurd.'

'I don't think so, I think it's Irma who's still bothering you.'

'You flatter yourself.'

'You know every well that if I'm friendly with someone else it doesn't make any difference to us.'

'Perhaps I'm envious,' Jean said. 'I'm not free to go around having fun like you, even if I wanted to, which I don't, not particularly.'

'Well, what are we arguing about?'

'It's not enough, Rick, to just *say* you love me.'

'You want action, not words.'

'Something like that,' she said. 'But all I'm asking at the moment is that you snap out of this depression.'

'I'm sorry,' he said, then spoilt the apology by adding: 'I'm sorry I'm the way I am, that's all I can say.'

They drove fast along the highway, then turned off down the dusty track to El Silencio. The sea looked very blue, flecked with white. There were people on the beach, but no one in the water. Rick parked the VW and found a comparatively isolated spot on the beach. Jean laid down the poncho and stretched out upon it.

'It's rough today,' Rick said. 'Look at those breakers.'

'I noticed that there was nobody swimming. If I were you I'd not go in beyond those first waves.'

'I'm not worried about a few breakers. In fact I think I'll go in for a while now.'

'Because I advised against it?'

'I just like a challenge.'

'And don't we all know it.'

But he didn't immediately head for the surf, Jean noticed. Instead he began to build a sandcastle for the children. From transistor radios nearby came a variety of programmes in Spanish. Jean watched the sunbathers clustered beneath the cliffs. They were lolling about like a colony of seals, stretched out for public display; sun-worshippers holding in their bellies and trying to become mahogany in colour. At times she felt there was something mindless, even distasteful about spending hours in the sun.

Rick finished his sandcastle and strolled down for a swim. Jean put aside her book for a moment and watched him.

'Be careful,' she shouted at his retreating back. The bay was turbulent with white horses all over and three lines of breakers – one close in to shore, another fifty yards out and a third stretching across from the point. She saw Rick dive through the first white wall and come up on the other side. He was swimming fast towards the second line. She watched him approach it. A wave rose up at least twenty feet and crashed down, but Rick was under it, swimming out into calmer water. For a moment she thought he was heading towards the breakers at the point, but two or three hundred yards off-shore he turned, swimming parallel to the beach. She watched him frog-kick through another turning wave and come out on the seaward side, a swimming goblin at this distance, his arms like the wings of a bird pointing towards the sky. Let it all go, she thought, depression, guilt, anger and jealousy. Let the sea take it like mothering flesh.

She stood up and collected the three children. They would go for a long walk, right to the far end of the beach so that when Rick came back he would have to search for them. Carrying David while the two girls tagged at her side, she strolled along the skirt of sand. Sara was collecting shells and at one point stopped and showed Jean a stranded starfish. She picked it up and threw it back into the water. Behind her she could see the blurred foothills. They were like soft suede animals at that distance.

Rick was fifteen minutes swim from shore, rising and falling on the swell when he first saw the fin. He lost sight of it as another roll of the sea pulled him into a trough between the waves. Mildly apprehensive he began to swim towards the beach. Rising on the swell again he saw the fin closer than before, the length of a cricket pitch away, between him and the yellowish cliffs. He kept watching it. There was no curve of back and it seemed smaller than a porpoise's. Involuntarily he gasped as if someone had punched him in the solar-plexus. For a moment he shut his eyes and the sun's glare through his eyelids created an infra-red cloud. Opening them he glanced round. The fin had disappeared. Then he saw it, behind him now. The temptation to panic was almost irresistible. Slow easy strokes, he thought, and no splashing.

He was swimming hard towards the second line of breakers, his breathing quick and irregular. As he could no longer see the fin Rick went under, half-turned in the opaque greenish water, but below the surface visibility was reduced to a few yards. Any moment he expected to see a sinister purplish-blue shape, a slender tail and the malevolent curve of its mouth. He breathed through his nose, choking a little as he swallowed some water, then hit the surface. He gulped in air and made a tremendous splash by accident. And saw the fin again. About fifteen yards off. In front of him, not too far away, were the breakers. He could hear their roar clearly now.

He dived under again. There was no shape or silhouette. Once again he rose to the surface and now he saw that the breakers were just in front of him. Panic overwhelmed him. Dropping all precaution he freestyled, legs going like pistons and making a white wake behind him. Then he was on the wave, lifted high, down, limbs out of control, swallowing water, upside-down, whirling like a piece of driftwood through the rush of the water. Before he had time for even a quick breath of air another breaker thumped down upon him. He had no idea where he was in relationship to the beach. For an instant he was in calm water, then another breaker rose up and crashed down. Thwacked by the wave, almost unable to breathe, he felt his lungs at bursting point. A fourth breaker hit him, tossed him up and threw him down in shallow water. He touched sand, stumbled, scrabbled forward, staggered two or three yards in the sludge, collapsed face down, his head buried in his arms. A handful of people crowded round him, bombarding him with questions. He looked up and saw Jean kneeling beside him. She put an arm round his waist and helped him to his feet. Her body felt warm against him.

He lit the cigarette Jean gave him, retched dryly and looked back at the sea, his eyes searching for the fin. There was no sign of it and he could have almost believed he'd imagined it.

'What happened?' Jean said. 'We thought you were never going to make it through those breakers.'

'I panicked,' he said. 'I saw this fin and I thought it was a shark.'

Jean laughed. 'It was probably a porpoise or a dolphin.'

'All I could think of was that blue shark we saw on the jetty at Chorrillos.' Though the sun was warm Rick was still trembling. He wrapped the poncho Jean had brought round his shoulders, lit another cigarette, put his arms round Sara and Emma. 'Probably I was in more danger of drowning in that sea.'

'Don't go that far out again.'

'I'll have to go for another swim before we leave,' Rick said. 'If only to get my confidence back.'

'Don't be silly,' Jean said. 'There's no one going in again after seeing you bouncing about on those breakers.'

Rick lay in the sun, his head in Jean's lap, feeling relief, all anxiety and guilt, all the negative emotions purged, exorcised. Never had he felt so content, so sane, lying on the soft sand in the warm sun. And he didn't go for another swim that day.

Julio Scorza had been arguing with some friends, expressing his disappointment in the revolution, protesting against their naive optimism. As Alberto had prophesied the months had passed and still no sweeping social measures were forthcoming. He had believed Peru to be on the threshold of change and all he had seen were increases in censorship and repression. Intellectuals had become a target for subtle propaganda. Writers who wrote simple lyrical stuff about their Indian heritage were applauded; those who attempted a more complex approach were attacked. Unambiguous patriotism was the order of the day and anything foreign was immediately suspect. And that included literary influences, especially American.

Feeling vaguely under threat Julio had been applying for posts abroad. A letter came from Arizona, offering him a post for the summer months as a visiting lecturer in Spanish literature. The salary was more than he could earn in a year in Lima. For the first time since he'd left home he would be financially independent. His delight was tempered only by the thought of Ana-Maria's reaction. He must call her.

'Guess what?' he said when she answered the phone.

'I don't know – what?'

'I've got that job in Phoenix.'

'Where's Phoenix?'

'Arizona, the south-west. I'll have to be leaving quite soon.'

'What are *we* going to do then?'

'Why don't you come and join me there as soon as I've found a place to live?'

'What about my parents, you know what they're like?'

'Look,' Julio said. 'We could get married.' The suggestion had slipped out in an unpremeditated way and immediately he felt a twinge of regret.

'Get married! There's a lot to talk about first. My family has never approved of us, you know that. I'm still at university and you won't really be able to support me. I don't know, Julio.'

'You don't want to?' Now he was a little piqued. He had expected Ana-Maria to jump at the opportunity. Although he had not told her so he imagined that her liberal ideas and professed emancipation were skin deep. A fashion, like Alberto's drugs and rock-music.

'I didn't say that,' she said. 'You've simply taken me by surprise, that's all. First the job in the States and now this. I'm not sure I like the idea of going to Arizona, and marriage requires a hell of a lot more consideration.'

'Ana, have dinner with me tonight? We'll talk about things then, OK?'

'That sounds a better idea.'

'I want to celebrate anyway. I'll call round about nine. We can go to a *Chifa*, I fancy some Chinese food.'

He heard her laugh lightly on the other end of the phone, then she rang off. He went to have a shower. He would go to the Haiti first, to savour the moment on his own and to quell the elation a bit with a few beers.

Chapter Seven

One Sunday towards the end of May Jean and Rick were having a picnic in a dry riverbed near Cieneguilla, Julio and Ana-Maria were sitting in the Odeon at Miraflores watching an Ingmar Bergman film, Cath was typing some translations in her study, Alberto, high on a joint, was lying back listening to a record by Pink Floyd, and Robert was making love to Sheila on their black sheets after they'd consumed two bottles of wine for lunch. Imperceptibly at first the white boulder upon which Rick was sitting began to vibrate. 'That's funny,' he said aloud, then heard a familiar rumbling sound and saw clouds of dust rolling down the hill slopes. The bamboo and ferns were swishing as if in a strong breeze. Julio noticed the screen begin to flicker. A fault, he thought, then heard someone scream. Cath stopped typing. The noise and movement increased in intensity. Cath remained rooted to her seat. The disruption of the sound, the odd jumping of the stylus on the stereo irritated Alberto. 'I need a new goddamn needle,' he said. 'Fuck it!' As the bed began to shake quite violently Robert thought for a moment that Sheila was having an unusually violent climax. Excited by the movement he came himself. Sheila was staring at him wide-eyed, unnaturally still.

'My God, let's get out of here!' Rick said. He grabbed Emma and Sara, ran to the bank, clambered up its steep side, began to stumble across a stretch of ploughed field. All around the earth was moving. Any moment he expected a fissure to appear in front of him. He wanted to run, but there was nowhere to run to. On the level ground he was at least safe from bouncing rocks which were by now crashing through the foliage on the far side of the stream.

'Alberto, do something!' Cath shrieked.

'I'm hallucinating,' he said, then noticed that the pictures on the walls were swinging erratically. A couple of books fell off a shelf.

'The kids are out somewhere,' Cath said. 'In the park, I think.'

'Sit where you are,' Julio said, grabbing Ana-Maria and holding her down. Around them people were screaming and scrambling for the exits. The screen was flickering wildly. Suddenly Sheila shrieked and jumped out of bed, tearing away from Robert.

'That hurt,' Robert said.

'You're crazy!' Sheila said and dashed to the window.

'Hurry up,' Rick shouted.

'Sit tight or get under the seat,' Julio urged.

'Don't panic,' Alberto said.

'I can't get up the bank,' Jean shouted. 'Come and help.' Rick ran back to the riverbed, lifted David over the top, stuck out a hand to Jean and pulled her up.

'I didn't realize it was a tremor,' Rick said.

'I thought it was the stylus,' Alberto said.

'I hope the kids are all right,' Cath said in a whisper.

'*El fin del mundo!*' shrieked Maria, the maid, running into the room.

'Just keep calm,' Julio said.

'I thought the earth moved for you *à la* Hemingway,' Robert said still laughing.

'You're an idiot!'

'I thought you were joking,' Jean said.

'It's subsiding now anyway,' Robert said.

'Must have lasted a couple of minutes,' Julio said.

'I lost all track of time.'

'Let's get back to the car,' Rick said. The VW was still intact. No boulders or rubble had crashed down upon it. Rick collected their things, packed them into the boot and began the journey to the city. Through the pass, a narrow canyon where the car was dwarfed by monolithic stone hills, he noticed a number of landslides strewn across the road, but none impeded him. Soon they were speeding on the downhill run towards the coast. Julio and Ana-Maria were walking towards the Haiti. The crowds were milling about in the streets, but they couldn't see much damage.

'I was petrified,' Ana-Maria said.

'You might have been trampled if we'd made for the exit,' Julio said.

'The kids have come home,' Cath said.

'Quite a screw,' Robert said and laughed again.

'I thought you'd gone out of your mind,' Sheila said.

'Wonder whether Lima's damaged,' Rick said. 'You know I still keep getting these premonitions that something'll stop us leaving this fucking place.'

Jean was silent. When the earthquake had started, the boulders clicking together like teeth, the slopes shaking off streams of stones and red dust, alarm had raced through her bloodstream like fire. That had been for the children. There was something so utterly claustrophobic about an earthquake, she thought, as if they were all standing inside a gigantic drum. She'd edged stiffly but calmly to the bank where Rick had helped her, then standing in the cane-stubble she'd felt a stab of pain in her right shoulder. It had made her wince.

'Just after I got into the field,' she said. 'I had this pain in my shoulder.'

'Probably a muscle.'

'It almost paralysed me for a moment and I keep wondering whether it's internal. In my lungs.'

'I shouldn't think so.'

'I keep remembering my father.'

'But, Jean, he was twenty years older than you are when he died. It was just a strained muscle.'

'I've had this bad cough ever since the weather got damper.'

'You should go and see the doctor about it,' Rick said. 'Get some antibiotic.'

'I'm scared.'

'Don't be silly. If you're the slightest bit worried, see the doctor.'

'I suppose I ought to if it doesn't improve.'

'It sounded like a lorry passing by,' Cath said. Alberto turned off his stereo and switched on TV. He wanted to watch the game, the first in the World Cup at Mexico City, Peru against Bulgaria. It was one of the reasons for his visit that afternoon though he hoped Cath wouldn't suspect this. Hoped too that the quake hadn't interfered with the programme. He'd been looking forward to seeing the fast and tricky Peruvian forwards run rings round the large and clumsy European defenders. Though he rarely praised things Peruvian, when it came to football Alberto was a fanatic.

'Turn off that television,' Cath said.

'Honey, it's the World Cup.'

'There's just been an earthquake and that's all you can think about.'

'Should be a good match.'

'Oh all right,' Cath said. 'Let football take precedence as usual.'

'Your face was glazed over like a mask,' Robert said.

'It's the hysteria that frightens me,' Julio said.

'I've been in them before,' Robert said. 'Last time I was in Plaza San Martín and the tramlines began to move like silver snakes.'

'It was during the *feria* for *El Señor de los Milagros*, the last one,' Julio said. 'And the following day the city was packed. There was some religious gathering, the air heavy with incense. A microphone relayed *Ave Marias* round the plaza and all the people, in their purple cassocks and rope belts, were praying and chanting.' He felt expansive, talking from sheer relief. 'They must have thought it was a sign from God. A personal message to warn them they were not taking their obligations seriously enough.'

'Don't be blasphemous,' Ana-Maria said smiling.

'All those people with their petty sins and small vices,' Julio elaborated. 'They thought it was an act of God. Terrifying though, the religious hysteria, almost violent in intensity. I was scared there would be another tremor.'

Rick was entering Miraflores and Jean was relieved to see their apartment still standing. Not long after they'd unpacked the car, had coffee and got the children a meal, Robert and Sheila called round. They invited them out for a drink. Rick drove to the *Haiti*. On the way long cavalcades of cars were hooting and blaring down the main avenue. Red and white flags were prominent. The sound of rattles was like machine-gun fire.

'Peru must have won again,' Rick said. He leaned out of the window and shouted to a passer-by. 'What was the score?'

'Peru won three-two.'

'Who scored?'

'Cubillas got two, Sotil the other.' Football triumphs and earthquakes on the same day, Rick thought, it was too much. The Haiti was crowded and buzzing with conversation. Robert spotted Julio and Ana-Maria in the far corner. They went across and sat down at the same table.

'It's been serious up in the north,' Julio told them. 'All the coastal towns have been flattened. The epicentre was out in the Pacific again, about two-hundred and fifty miles north.'

'I must go up there tomorrow,' Robert said. 'And check it out.'

'I'll come with you,' Julio said. 'My parents live near Chimbote and I'm worried about them. Couldn't get through on the phone, although that's nothing unusual.'

'Incidentally,' Ana-Maria said, smiling and putting her hand over Julio's. 'We've got some personal news to tell you.'

'Yes,' Julio said. 'We're thinking of getting married.'

'Well, congratulations.'

'You see, I've been offered a job for the summer, lecturing at Arizona State University in Phoenix, and we both want to go so I suppose we'll have to put our relationship on a more conventional basis. To satisfy Ana-Maria's parents.'

Robert laughed. 'Come on, Julio,' he said. 'I find it hard to believe. You're going to the States? That land of economic imperialism? That decadent capitalist society?'

'I want to see it for myself,' Julio said.

'They're going to pay him three thousand dollars for the summer semester,' Ana-Maria said. Robert laughed again.

'I'll be able to sow discord and dissent from the inside,' Julio said, but smiled ruefully.

'They won't let you in if they know you're a communist.'

'I've never been a member of the Party,' Julio said. 'I'm a Marxist. Besides, I'm a poet. My function is to record reality as I see it. Through the microscope of my peculiar and unique vision,' he added laughing too. 'I'm above politics and toe no party line. I do what I want and go where I like.'

'OK, OK,' Robert said. 'You're a poet, not a political animal.'

Paradise of Exiles

'I'd have preferred Berkeley or somewhere, but as an underprivileged denizen of the Third World I'm not in a position to choose.'

'You should have a good time in Arizona,' Robert said. 'But I still can't imagine it. Julio Scorza in the States.'

'Yes,' Julio said. 'I should give thanks to the tainted money that makes it possible. It probably comes from exploitation of Peru anyway.'

'And offering you a post is their means of disarming you,' Robert said. 'Traducing your integrity. I know, I've heard you say so.'

'*Dios*, Robert, you certainly go on. In fact you're getting boring ... Anyway, I'm having a party on the eve of our flight into Egypt, the land of milk and honey, and you're all invited.'

Robert and Julio travelled to Chimbote the following day, shocked by the news they'd heard over the radio that morning. An avalanche had followed the quake in the valley of Huarás and several towns had been buried beneath a mass of mud, ice, sludge and shale from the mountains. Casualty estimates were rising with each news bulletin. Food and water were severely limited and though helicopters were trying to reach the valley it was still cut off. They met a reporter at a town outside Lima who had flown over the area. From the plane all he'd been able to see were the crests of some palm trees and church spires above the mud.

Hemmed in by jagged hunks of cliff, a boomtown flourishing on fishmeal manufactured in factories near the docks and surrounded by shanties, Chimbote was now in ruins. A pall of dust hung over the entire town. They booked in at the main hotel, then Robert went off to see if he could get up into the sierra while Julio set out in search of his parents. With a sense of foreboding he wandered through the ruins. His parents' house was still standing. He found his father helping some neighbours to sort and sift through the rubble, rescuing blankets, furniture and personal belongings. Pigeons and seagulls whirled overhead. Stray dogs sniffed and whined round the ruins. His parents' account of the previous afternoon was fragmentary. They'd been at a church fete when it occurred. Many of the people had thought there was going to be a tidal wave and had panicked. Even now they were still in a state of shock.

Julio stayed for dinner, urging his parents to return to Lima with him, but they were worried that their house would be looted if they did. Returning after a few drinks with his father, Julio found Robert in the hotel bar. He'd been unable to get a lift into the mountains. Only military and medical personnel were being allowed through. Journalists were being refused entry. There weren't sufficient helicopters, they were told, but Robert thought it was a deliberate attempt to censor information.

They stayed another day, Robert interviewing survivors and accumulating information, Julio wandering through the port with his father, besieged by memories of his childhood when he'd watched the fishing-boats sail at dawn, cutting through the blue bay towards the open sea, envious of the men on board. They were a tough breed who collected in the smoke-filled bars of the town and told him far-fetched versions of their adventures. The dust, desert sun, sticky tarmac of the streets and the odour of fishmeal brought it all back to him. He could remember the jaded faces of the factory-owners, friends of his father, discussing profits. The main theme of their conversation was always money and the possibility of making a fortune.

Once on a hot day in June Julio had witnessed the break-up of a fishermen's strike. They'd gathered in clusters on streetcorners, the corrugated roofs above them gleaming in the sun. From a hill of shale, the grey islands and greenish sea to his left, Julio had watched the men's final struggle with the police on the bridge across the harbour. The two groups had jostled together in the heat, trading punches, sweaty faces bobbing up and down, the police suddenly retreating to the far end. In their drab green uniforms, automatic-rifles at their hips, they'd looked sinister in the crystal sunlight. Four times the fishermen had charged, trying to break police ranks, and each time a volley of shots was fired. After the fourth attempt the crowd slowly dispersed, leaving five of their number dead on the bridge. Even now Julio could recall the stray shouts, the screams and the pools of congealing blood on the concrete. And that night the town had remained awake, disturbed by the high-pitched wailing of bereaved women. It was Julio's first encounter with the brutality of authority. Until then he'd been a typical middle-class lad, unthinking and privileged. Afterwards

Paradise of Exiles

he'd become something of a radical, determined to work for justice and equality. Now ten years later, nothing had changed. Chimbote lay in ruins and he himself was off to the States for the summer. There was little, it seemed, that he or anyone who shared his convictions could do to help.

When they finally left, driving through the devastated streets for the last time, Julio recalled his adolescent friend, Red, a mulatto with strangely-chestnut hair. Together they'd played football on the yellow sand, churning it into a treacle, gone swimming, wandered round the oily port getting into mischief, sweating in the shimmering heat. Red had continually joked and boasted about his prowess with the girls. He'd wanted to play football for Peru, but had almost certainly become a fisherman or a worker in one of the factories, married perhaps, with half-a-dozen kids, his weakness for alcohol indulged when wages were high, nursing his dreams and ambitions. Julio decided not to look him up. Let his images remain intact. All impressions then had been so sharp, so final. The nights thick and sweet like honey; dance-halls, havens of gleaming thighs; girls' bodies quick and soft and palpitating; his adolescent lusts, a slow fever like fire running through the bloodstream; the hills above the town, chiselled stone and always the sea in the background, a gleam of metal, a blue dye . . .

Back in Lima Robert published his impressions of the earthquake in the *Herald* and was astonished when the editor told him a week later that his article had been syndicated throughout the Americas. It brought in nearly a thousand dollars. He and Sheila began to make their plans to leave Peru. Robert wrote to the various editors who'd published his article and though their answers were cautious, one, a monthly dealing with unusual phenomena, natural disasters and science at a popular level, appeared to promise more. Robert made copies of his *Herald* articles and forwarded them. The editor wrote back assuring him of a job, at least on a part-time basis. They could leave at last.

The party on the eve of Julio's departure for Arizona was held in the luxury apartment of his publisher, a middle-aged lady who owned vast estates in the south and who seemed to know little about contemporary

105

poetry in any language though she spoke several fluently. She'd published Julio's last book because it had won a national poetry prize in manuscript. All the young writers paid her a good deal of polite attention. Even Julio was courteous and less-opinionated than usual. There was a succulent buffet – diced turkey, plates of spicy Creole food, lobster salad, strawberries and icecream, gateaux, and a variety of imported cheeses. Indian waiters came round with a continuous supply of *pisco* sours and Scotch. It was a small irony, Rick thought, that half the writers there were Marxists.

After the rich food had disappeared, rather rapidly he noticed, everyone sat around amongst the expensive bric-a-brac and the abstract paintings, listening to various poets reading selections of their recent work. Then someone played gaucho music on a guitar, a virtuoso display that went on for a solid hour, but became tedious after the first ten minutes. Rick listened to interminable discussions on white magic in the sierra, apothecaries, quack healers, herbalists and astrology. He overheard bits of a debate on free love, a long argument defining pornography and another on the ambiguity of language. Wealthy patrons of the arts described the barbarity of the racial crisis in the USA and the war in Vietnam. Jean had been wise to stay away. Leaving Cath to hold the fort with the intellectuals he went off in search of Alberto.

He bumped into Irma looking as sexy as ever. She introduced him to the young man she was with, an Indian poet from Cuzco. Rick felt a small stab of jealousy, dismissed it, smiled as nonchalantly as possible and drew her aside for a moment.

'Look,' he said. 'When are we going to see each other again?'

'We're not,' she said. 'I told you, except as friends, and I hope we can be that. I'm looking forward to your lectures on Byron.'

'Did I tell you I swam too far out one afternoon and nearly got drowned? Because I wanted to see you and was feeling depressed.'

She laughed. 'I don't believe a word of it, but I'm sure you'll find solace and consolation somewhere. The trouble with you, Rick, is that you're too open. You talk about things too much and try to shock people.'

'You mean I lack subtlety?'

'Something like that.'

Later he found Alberto sorting through the records by the stereo. 'It's a drag, this party,' Alberto said. 'Haven't even got any Stones or Beatles.'

'I'm out of my element,' Rick said.

'Let's cut out.'

'I'll just say goodbye to Julio.'

Julio was talking to Robert. The fact that they were both leaving Peru seemed to have revitalised their friendship. Rick felt betrayed in a peculiar way. All his friends abandoning the sinking ship. Even Cath was making arrangements to take her children to the States. Only he, Jean and Alberto would be left. All those people who had persuaded him to return; who had collected around him during a more affluent period; they were all going. It was a subtle treachery. What was his future? A downward spiral into middle-age.

'Give me a joint,' he said to Alberto when they were sitting in his VW outside. 'I need it.' Irma's words lingered in his mind like a reproach. He talked too much. He was indiscreet. Well, he would have to change. Build up some armour-plated defence. Become more self-contained and independent.

Alberto said 'I'm off to Tarma in July, to get some cocaine, then I'm going on to San Ramón on the edge of the jungle. Would you like to come?'

'I certainly would.'

'You know,' Alberto said. 'Cathy's itching to get away and if she leaves the kids I won't be able to piss off to the sierra all the time. Goddamn, I should never have got married, man. I'm an irresponsible bastard, I suppose, certainly not prepared to knuckle down and provide some mythical state of security for a family – which is what Cath's searching for.'

'Perhaps we're both out of step.'

'We're no different from anyone else,' Alberto said. 'Everyone wants to live out their fantasies.'

'I read somewhere that only psychopaths try to actually live out all their fantasies.'

'We're all goddamn psychopaths then.'

'It's just that we don't, or won't play the roles expected of us. We don't pretend.'

'Let's drive down to the sea-front.'

They stopped on the promenade at Miraflores. The shale cliffs plunged away beneath them and looking across the bay they could see the lines of surf, white foam curdling round the rocks.

'Ever felt the urge to jump?' Alberto said.

'I may be self-destructive, but I'm not suicidal. I knew that when I was being tossed about in those breakers the other week. Nothing was sweeter than lying on the wet sand, the taste of salt water and vomit in my mouth.'

'There's a difference, I suppose, between taking calculated risks and actually killing oneself,' Alberto said. 'You know, Rick, if I'm honest I've got to admit I took Cath too much for granted. I didn't realize how much I needed her until we split.'

'It's not the end of things.'

'Perhaps the separation will be good for us.'

'And perhaps you'll meet someone else.'

'Or she will,' Alberto said. 'The irony is I didn't know it would hurt so much. She said to me, go if you must and I went, and now she's the one who seems glad to be alone and I'm the one who's hurt.'

'She's probably hurt too, I'm sure she must be. It's always a painful process when two people who've been together for a long time separate.'

'I want it both ways,' Alberto said. 'I don't like to be alone, but I don't like the restrictions of marriage either.'

'There's no answer or solution,' Rick said. 'Let's go to the Haiti and have a few beers.'

'Yeah, this is good grass, man. I feel pretty high already.'

Chapter Eight

The early morning was misty and drizzle dampened the streets when Alberto and Rick started on their trip to Tarma. Rick had a heavy cold and sinus trouble. With Alberto driving they were soon in the foothills, the road winding parallel to the Rio Rimac which bubbled along below them, brown and frothy cream. Once above the cloudbelt they were in the sun, old Inca terraces lacing the mountains, a condor hovering between peaks, a yellow and green train zigzagging like a caterpillar above them or disappearing into one of the tunnels forged through the solid rock.

By midday they were at the top of the pass, sixteen-thousand feet above sea-level. Snowcapped peaks, barren rock streaked with maroon, gunmetal, rust and verdigris, the cold ice-blue of the lakes, and the satanic gloom of mills and mines a little lower down. Alberto stopped for a few minutes. The air was chilled and breathing a little more difficult. Rick took over the wheel and they began the descent across the *altiplano* – coarse grass, a splash of mauve and orange flowers in clumps, long-necked solemn-looking llamas grazing, a blustery wind.

They stopped at a roadside cafe, had some stew and coffee, then continued. As they emerged through the pass, range upon range of mountains turning mauve in the distance, they could see the town below them, a mass of redroofed houses snug in a checkerboard valley of yellows, russets, browns. The road spiralled in wide loops down, Rick taking it slowly in second gear.

It was almost dusk when they arrived. They tried to book in at the Tourist Hotel but it was full, so they checked in at a cheap pension in a sidestreet. Rick had a slight headache. After a shower he lay down on the narrow single-bed, hoping it would ease off, but instead it got worse. A blinding pressure behind the eyes, a hammering in the skull. Alberto knocked on his door, came in.

'Are you ready?' he asked. 'Let's go over to the Tourist Hotel and have a drink.'

'I feel terrible,' Rick said. 'I've got this headache like a migraine. I must find a *farmacia* and get some aspirin.'

'Do you feel dizzy and a bit nauseous?'

'I feel lousy.'

'It's *soroche* – mountain sickness. Remember we're ten thousand feet up here.'

'I've never had it before,' Rick said. 'I thought it was a bit of a myth. Psychosomatic and all that.'

'It's real enough. Probably hit you badly because you've got a cold. Come on, we'll go and get something for it.'

At the Tourist Hotel Alberto ordered beer for himself, lemon tea and four aspirin tablets for Rick. 'Here,' he said. 'Take these. Don't touch any alcohol tonight, it'll make things worse.'

'It's so bad I feel as though I'm in some sort of trance.'

'You'll be fine tomorrow. Best thing is to have an early night. I've got to see one or two people. You go back to the pension. Sleep it off.'

Rick finished his tea and left. He walked back through the dark streets, went to his room, undressed, tried to sleep. He lay on the brass-knobbed rickety bed in the bare room staring at the bluewashed ceiling and the naked electric light, scarcely able to breathe, the blood pounding in his head. 'Jesus,' he murmured almost in tears with the pain, his chest tight as if someone had encased him in constricting armour. He thought of Jean and the kids back in Lima and wondered what had possessed him to leave the safety of the coast. He had never felt so alone in his life. His breathing became quick and difficult. Anxiety increased his breathlessness. He was almost too scared to sleep. The bloody irony, he thought. To have survived revolution, an earthquake and a drowning (well, almost a drowning) only to die of *soroche* in a godforsaken town in the sierra.

At last he dropped off into a fitful sleep, only to be awoken by Alberto who returned about midnight.

'How're you feeling, man?' he asked.

Paradise of Exiles

'Terrible,' Rick said. 'I thought I was going to kick it. I could hardly breathe.'

Alberto laughed. 'You'll be all right in the morning. Try and get some sleep.' Rick could tell that Alberto had been smoking marijuana. He was calmly amused by Rick's *soroche*.

'Don't know how you've got the nerve to smoke a joint at this altitude.'

'It's good for you,' Alberto said. 'You'll be high tomorrow, sure thing. Anyway, I got some *coke* this evening. Good business. You want a sniff? It might clear that head of yours.'

'I want to sleep. I'll see you in the morning if I survive the night.' Alberto left, chuckling. 'It's all right, for you,' Rick said. 'Go on, have a good laugh.' Alberto did.

Rick rolled back and fell into a restless sleep. Sometime during the early hours he was awoken by a familiar rumbling sound as if a ten-ton truck were passing underneath the floorboards. He switched on the light. The walls were shaking, the light bulb swinging. A fucking tremor, he thought, but didn't budge. He dropped off to sleep again. In the morning he got up somewhat gingerly in case his head was still thumping, but discovered it felt fine. He recalled his fears of the night and laughed.

'There was a tremor during the night,' Alberto said at breakfast. 'Did you feel it?'

'I thought it was a figment of my paranoia.'

'A lot of people ran out into the street, but it didn't last long. I was so high I just lay there grinning.'

They went out and wandered round the rancid-smelling market, the alleys rivulets of slime, a black treacle underfoot. It was raining steadily. A man dressed in sacks, his feet bare, begged for a few *soles*. All the Indian women on the pavement, selling vegetables, fruit, llama-skin rugs, ponchos, beads and bowler hats, had V-shaped frown-lines, even the younger ones, though it was difficult to determine their age. Anxiety and chronic insecurity had blurred the usual distinctions.

'When I look round at these people,' Rick said. 'It makes me feel that all my depressions are neurotic.'

'There's a kind of melancholy pervades these small towns,' Alberto

111

said. 'Nothing's changed for centuries. Sometimes I can't believe the people are quite real. They're so alien they become part of the scenery. For us tourists to dig.'

'When you look closer and see their concern for their children,' Rick said, 'you suddenly realize they're human and it's a shock.'

'And living at subsistence level,' Alberto said. 'Yes, makes our worries those of sophisticated goddamn westerners. Who cares if your wife leaves you and takes the kids when you're starving? You're better off. Who cares about relationship and the rest of it when you've got a goddamn hole in your belly?'

'All you want is your *pisco*, temporary oblivion.'

'And at that level we meet,' Alberto said. 'After all we're smoking grass and looking for cocaine. That's all I want.'

'We're after new experience. We're seeking to stimulate our jaded senses. We want shifts of emotion for kicks. Not on the same level at all. These poor sods want to numb sensation. We want to sharpen it.'

'I don't,' Alberto said. 'Let's go on to San Ramón tomorrow morning. I'm trying to get hold of this drug, *ayahuascar*. It's an hallucinogen that the jungle Indians use. Ginsberg tried it when he was here.'

'Fine,' Rick said.

That evening they went to a fiesta in a nearby village. It was pitch black when they arrived, Indian families emerging from the darkness, high-spirited and laughing. Everyone was going to a firework display in the plaza. Thin drizzle was falling and though the fireworks fizzled out and the catherine-wheels got stuck no one seemed to mind. They went on to a huge candle-lit barn. All of the locals were drunk. Women served food on the patio and the men in their ponchos and broadrimmed hats were drinking. Alberto rolled a joint and Rick smoked it despite his fear of the altitude. Drinking appeared to be a ritual. Everyone dipped their mugs into the huge vat of *chicha*, thick brown liquor running over hands and fingers, then invited someone else to sip from their mug. After several such invitations Alberto and Rick began to get into the mood of the gathering.

Later everyone danced. Skirts swirled and handkerchiefs were twirled. The music got progressively louder as sad Indian laments were replaced by the more abandoned dances of the coast. Rick and Alberto danced

Paradise of Exiles

with most of the local girls who made a fuss of the two blue-jeaned *gringos* unexpectedly in their midst. There was chicken and rice, potatoes in a spicy cheese sauce, guinea pig – a delicacy, and vegetables spiced with red peppers. The party was going to continue until the dawn, but as they were travelling the following day Alberto and Rick had to leave.

Leaving Tarma at midday Rick drove fast along an avenue lined with eucalyptus trees until he hit the corkscrew pass. It followed the river which shone like a piece of tin-foil below them. As he cornered the precipitous drops were only inches from the off-side wheels. In fifty miles they dropped eight-thousand feet and were level with the stream, waterfalls and cascades sliding like mercury down the slopes of green jungle. They stopped and stripped off coats and sweaters. The road straightened out through low-lying hills into San Ramón, an L-shaped ramshackle town on the river. Rick and Alberto booked in at the Tourist Hotel, then went off for a meal.

After they'd eaten they drank at various bars and were directed to a variety of people who lived in shacks along the waterfront, but Alberto had little luck in his quest for *ayahuascar*. Each shack they visited seemed identical, with a camp-bed in a dark corner, a Sacred Heart on the wall next to calendars advertising Coca Cola, a tin roof and a clutter of cooking utensils, but no sign of drugs. Returning to the hotel they played poker and smoked marijuana for a couple of hours before going to sleep. Next morning they moved on to Pampasilva, a village on the Perené – a tributary of the Amazon. The road was narrow, unmetalled, greasy with red mud, scored by the indentations of tyre-tracks and crumbling away on the open side. Below were the usual steep drops to the river which they crossed and re-crossed by means of rickety bridges. A couple of hours out of San Ramón all traffic was halted. Alberto and Rick got out and walked alongside the line of trucks and buses to investigate. It was very hot and the sounds of the jungle loud all round them.

As they rounded a corner they saw what had happened. A little crowd had gathered and were gazing down. A pick-up truck had gone over the edge. The dense vegetation had pinned it to the slope about fifty yards down. The women and children who had been in the back and thrown out were being helped up with ropes. They were bedraggled and covered in cuts and abrasions. One of the women was screaming hysterically. Alberto questioned someone in the crowd.

'It happened ten minutes ago,' he told Rick. 'The bloke driving and his mate are still trapped in the cab.'

'Shit!' Rick said. Sunlight sparkled on green leaves. The whine of the insects was continuous. 'Let's go down and see if we can help.'

'The cops are on their way,' Alberto said.

A few minutes later the police arrived and called for volunteers. Alberto and Rick scrambled down the bank with tow-ropes. It took them half-an-hour, stripped to the waist and sweating, to move the truck. The driver had tried to leap through the open window and was trapped with the weight of the truck across his chest. His companion was unconscious in the cab. All the time they were heaving on the ropes, the trapped man was talking to them. He couldn't feel any pain, he said, only an intense pressure. He was sure he was going to be all right. He kept thanking them for their help. Once they'd lifted the truck sufficiently a policeman carefully pulled the man clear. He was smiling, but as Rick watched he went white and made an odd gurgling sound. Blood haemorrhaged from his mouth. Within seconds he was dead. They strapped the body to a piece of canvas and levered it up the slope, then rescued his friend. He was unconscious, but breathing. The police took him back to San Ramón in their landrover.

'Give me a cigarette,' Rick said. They sat on the mud bank, smoking. They were both shaken. One of the women was still shrieking at intervals. The traffic had begun to move.

'Let's go on,' Alberto said.

They drove slowly down the winding road which became muddier and more treacherous as they descended. At Pampasilva, a collection of huts on the river, they went straight to the only bar, a wooden shack on stilts above the water, and drank six bottles of beer each. Afterwards Alberto made a few enquiries about *ayahuascar*, but without enthusiasm or success.

'Let's go back before sunset,' Alberto said. 'I don't fancy that drive in the dark.'

'I can't get over that bloke,' Rick said. 'I'd no idea he was that badly hurt.'

'Must have been bleeding internally. Put the incident into a poem and forget it.'

'Shit, man!'

'There are only two subjects for poetry – love and death, aren't there? I've heard you say so.'

'It could have been us.'

'Sure. It can happen any bloody time. Thank God you never know when.'

'Let's get back to Lima.'

'Yeah, and sell that *coke*. I had a momentary fear when we were helping the police about all the stuff in our car. Christ, it takes an incident like that to bring you down to basics.'

'How do you mean?'

'Survival . . . Funny though, as we were driving down I kept thinking about Cathy. I thought separation would sort things out, but it's not worked like that. She's still bitter and wants to go ahead with the divorce.' They were driving alone the same muddy track, the sky in the west pink-flushed as the sun went down, the mountainous jungle serene and beautiful. 'She says we've re-created nothing,' Alberto said. 'That we – she really means me – were simply not brave enough. That unless there are sacrifices and compromises there's no marriage. I've failed, she says, and our marriage has failed. It takes courage to stick together and I was prepared to ditch our relationship for the sake of my own fulfilment. I've lost everything, she claims, and will go on losing everything because I'm a selfish bastard. We've just been living in a kind of limbo, she told me.'

'What do you want yourself?'

'I don't know,' Alberto said. 'Like I told you, I want it both ways. I want my freedom and I want Cathy. It seems I can't have both. I've got to make some sort of choice. Well, if she wants out, if she wants to go to the States, let her. That's what I say. The world's full of women, at least I've found that out. Trouble is, none of them turn me on, emotionally I mean. Still they're some consolation.'

'The sweet solace of flesh . . .'

115

'You can put it like that, but the strange thing is, Rick, I often used to envy those guys who were on their own. I thought their lives were full of excitement and novelty, but it's not like that at all. Five or six nights a week I'm on my own. Sometimes longer. It takes some getting used to, I can tell you.'

'Well, we're all on our own finally.'

'Easy to say that, man, when you're living with Jean. Not so easy when you're actually alone to get much consolation from it, but I'll get used to it, I suppose.'

They left San Ramón at dawn the following day. The jungle was veiled in mist, the distant hills bluish-mauve. Rick caught a tang of wet earth and the aroma of woodsmoke from a nearby plantation. They could hear gunshots in the hills. Someone must have been out hunting. Learning to live alone was an essential part of growing up, Rick thought, though he didn't say so to Alberto. He was by no means sure that he had learnt that lesson himself.

By midday they were up on the high plateau, an icy wind knifing through their sweaters, and in the afternoon were driving through a snowstorm at the top of the pass, the road lassoing through a no-man's-land of mineral-coloured peaks and cold grey lakes. The exhaust pipe fell off the car one rough section of the road. They crouched down in the blizzard, teeth chattering, trying to wrench it off completely after an unsuccessful attempt to strap it up with their belts. By early evening they were speeding through the hills towards the city. They could see its red glow though the coast was still covered in mist. Rick was glad to get back to Jean and the children.

Jean crossed the plaza in front of their apartment block, pushing David in his pram. The grass was yellow and desiccated, the path thick with dust. Just before she reached the far side a red setter came bounding over to greet her. It sniffed at David and Jean laughed at his huge delight. The girls wanted a dog, they kept on about it. Perhaps a red setter or a dalmatian. She had promised Sara one when they returned to England, imagining at that moment the house they would buy. On the coast perhaps, near cliffs covered in gorse and fern. The previous afternoon Rick had returned. He had played with the kids, pleased to

Paradise of Exiles

be home after his trip. He'd listened to his Bob Dylan records, Sara on one knee, Emma on the other. Jean had watched their three heads together – gold, copper and brown – as Rick had told them about the donkeys in the streets of Tarma and various cats they'd had as pets in the past. A Dutch interior, she'd thought, a pleasing domestic scene. One of their good times. Cats were lucky. They'd certainly have another when they got a place of their own. She visualised herself in the turquoise and green waistcoat Rick had bought for her, sitting on a large rug in front of a log fire, a marmalade cat purring on the armchair, the room darkening, firelight and snow outside, Rick telling the kids stories of his travels and she sketching pictures for them, sipping a glass of mulled wine, the sound of the sea in the distance and the wind moaning in pine trees outside . . .

As she crossed Paseo de la Republica towards the shops she saw two kites circling high in the grey sky above the arid hills that merged into cloud.

'I'm getting more and more homesick,' she said to David, looking forward to that day when they would be leaving, sailing on a cargo boat for Europe. She was tiring of this exile that forced them into themselves, tired of being isolated by language and culture. In her mind she saw their car dwarfed and vulnerable, surrounded by masses or rock a million years old, immutable. An image retained from a recent drive they had taken. She smiled at David, shivered slightly and had a momentary fear that they would never leave this country. Never see England again. And with the fear she felt a stab of pain in her left shoulder.

She walked on down to the sea-front, the ocean dark grey, the horizon invisible in heavy mist, the crumbling hunks of cliff, shale falling away to the pebbly beach, flat-roofed houses stretching back towards the shops. Suddenly she picked David up from the push-chair, hugged him, holding him with a possessive desperation almost like a tearing of her flesh, a birth pang. Reluctantly she put him down. He smiled and she continued towards the supermarket. There was food to buy, a meal to be cooked. She would give the children scrambled eggs and make something more interesting for Rick when he came back from his evening lecture.

117

Returning the quick way, a bag full of groceries over the push-chair, she saw Cath, slim in jeans, hurrying over to her parked VW. It was almost dusk and the pavements crowded with people on their way home, the traffic hooting and screeching as it braked at the lights.

'Hi,' Cath called catching sight of Jean. 'Let met give you a lift.'

They piled into the car, the folded push-chair and bag of groceries on the backseat. 'I've just been to the post,' Cathy said. 'There was a letter from that publisher. They've accepted the anthology. I was just coming over to tell Rick about it.'

'That's tremendous,' Jean said. It did indeed seem good news that the book the three of them had been working on since their return to Lima had been taken. The best news she had had in months. 'Stay for some dinner,' Jean said. 'Rick won't be back until later. He's teaching.'

'I'll phone the maid and tell her to give the children something to eat and make sure they get to bed,' Cath said. 'Let me buy some beer. We should celebrate tonight.'

Cath helped Jean bring her shopping up the lift, then they sat down at the kitchen table, poring over the contract. Jean made some coffee. Standing on the veranda she could see that the mist had cleared. Out on the steel sea the mauve off-shore islands were now visible and the sky was flecked with high cirrus cloud.

'Listen,' Cath said. 'I think I will go home first and make sure the kids are OK. I just remembered that Alberto's coming round for an hour.'

'How is he?'

'Haven't seen him since he returned from Tarma, but I imagine he enjoyed the trip.'

'Rick seemed to have done, but he was glad to be back.'

Cath laughed. 'I don't think Alberto is as happy as he expected to be on his own. No one to cook for him, to wash his shirts or make sure he gets up in time for work. Until he went to Tarma I'd seen more of him than I had done for ages. He misses the kids.'

'It's ironic, I suppose.'

'The really ironic thing is that I'm enjoying my independence more than I expected. No man to worry about. I can live alone, I've discovered that. It was that state of limbo when I hardly saw him, but never knew whether he'd be home or not, that I found hard to take.'

'He's been like a bear with a sore head,' Jean said, 'everytime I've seen him. I'm sure he's missing you.'

'He's missing all those little things I did for him and which he took for granted.'

'I know what you mean. A few days away and Rick came home all appreciative and uxorious.'

'Well,' Cath said. 'You know what they say, don't you?'

'What?'

'They say women get hard and men get cynical.'

'Maybe, but we shouldn't get all wound up tonight. I'm delighted about the book and I know Rick will be over the moon.'

'I'll be back in a couple of hours,' Cath said. 'We'll get drunk, I think we deserve some relaxation.'

'I was feeling quite homesick until I saw you this afternoon.'

Cath smiled. 'Be back later,' she said.

Jean waved to her from the balcony and began to prepare the meal. A few minutes later Sara and Emma came bursting in with Isolina, the Indian maid, who had taken them on their tricycles to the park. The next two hours would be hectic, Jean knew, but she was looking forward to the celebrations later.

Chapter Nine

Robert's last assignment for the *Herald* was to interview an American film actress, Sharon Winthrop, who had been on location near Cuzco. When he visited her at the Hotel Bolivar he found to his irritation that she was staying with a French film-extra, Pierre, who looked a little like Alain Delon. Sharon wasn't well-known herself, but she'd been working for a famous director who was still shooting in the small town he'd virtually hired for his film. She had long brown hair and a really tremendous figure. All the time he was plying her with questions about her career, ambitions and background, she moved restlessly round the room, her shape in the faded-blue, tight-denim of her jeans mobile, voluptuous. He found it difficult to avoid staring at her.

When he'd finally finished, Sharon asked him if he had anything to smoke. Robert offered her a cigarette.

'No, I mean grass,' she said. 'Marijuana.'

'I haven't, Robert said, 'but I know some people who might have. If you and Pierre aren't busy this evening, I'll take you round to meet them.'

'That would be great,' she said smiling.

Jean was cooking when they arrived and she invited them to stay for supper. Sharon chatted to Rick while Sheila went into the kitchen to help Jean. Sharon told him about the film they'd been shooting in the sierra and mentioned the various places they'd visited.

'Cuzco was a real funny little place,' she said. 'The people just gawped at us all the time. We all smoked marijuana in the Tourist Hotel at night and no one gave a good goddamn. They must have decided we were too big a gold mine to worry about little things like infringing their narcotic laws.'

'That's one of the reasons I brought Sharon round,' Robert said.

'She'd like to get hold of some pot and I thought you might have some. If not, perhaps we could call on Alberto.'

'Robert's told me all about you and Alberto,' Sharon said. 'You're a poet and you're both into drugs, right? He said you smuggled dope across the frontier from Colombia. Colombian gold, I imagine. Well, our supply has dried up and we want to turn-on with some people who are *simpatico*.'

'Robert's been exaggerating as usual,' Rick said. 'Actually I'm in Peru as a teacher – just to keep the record straight. And as for marijuana – I haven't got any here, but Alberto's bound to have a bit.'

'Sounds real groovy,' Sharon said. 'Tell me what sort of poetry you write.'

'Sexy stuff,' Robert said chuckling. 'I interviewed him once for the *Herald* and he said it was all about relationship.'

'I said the poetry came from the people I was around and that I liked.'

'And loved.'

'I meant Jean and the kids and you and Alberto and Cathy. All my friends.'

'I'd dig reading some,' Sharon said. 'I was at a reading in San Francisco just before we flew out here. It was wild.'

'Who was reading?'

'Oh I forget now. I'm not really into poetry. Folk and rock are more my scene – Janis Joplin, Joni Mitchell, they're the greatest. I dig Allen Ginsberg too. People like that.'

'Put some of your Dylan records on,' Robert said. 'And I'll go and get some beer.'

'In the fridge,' Rick said. Robert went into the kitchen and Rick followed. 'Where did you meet Sharon?' he asked. 'She's beautiful.'

'Thought you'd fancy her,' Robert said. 'The paper put me on to her. Told me to get an interview. Evidently she's been in several films. I've got her address and I'm going to look her up when I get to the States.'

Rick poured out some beer, handed the glasses round, and put a record on. Jean took Sharon to see the children who were sleeping. In a few minutes they were back, Sharon enthusing about the kids.

'When are you going back to the States?' Rick asked.

'In a few days,' she said. 'Pierre is going on to Paris. He's got a small part in some film there.'

'Wish I could get to the States,' Rick said. 'I've had enough of it here, but I've got to stay until my contract ends.'

'Well, you seem to have things pretty well set up here. It's free and easy and you have plenty of friends.'

'It's just that I reckon California is the best place to be at the moment, especially if you write the sort of stuff I do,' Rick said. 'It's funny, but I don't get homesick for England, not really, I've got this nostalgia for San Francisco and I've never even been there. I suppose it's all the films I've seen and the books I've read. Anyway, Lima's so parochial. I sometimes long for a big cosmopolitan city where you can do exactly what you want yet remain anonymous. If you see what I mean.'

'I dig it here,' Sharon said. 'It's so uncomplicated. No hassles, no one trying to rip you off all the time. I've never felt up-tight here.'

'That's because you're really a tourist. Believe me, it's screwed up and it infects you in the end. I have this idea of the West Coast being liberal and progressive.'

'People have their hang-ups everywhere.'

'It's not to escape my hang-ups that I want to leave,' Rick said. 'I suppose it's just that I miss an English-speaking community. That gets you from time to time. I've been too long in the same place and sometimes I feel it's the wrong place.'

'What about your wife?'

'She likes it here. She was the one who persuaded me to come back. Now she wants to return to England, get a house there and settle down a bit. We've been nomadic for years.'

'With the children, I can understand that. But if you ever do land up in LA, you're welcome to visit.'

'Thanks.'

'What about going to see your friend – Alberto?'

As they were leaving, Jean suggested that they brought Alberto back for dinner. Rick drove into the centre of Miraflores and as Alberto's apartment was close by parked in front of the Haiti.

'Let's have a quick beer first,' he said.

'OK,' Sharon said smiling. In the cafe it seemed to Rick that several people kept staring at Sharon, then as they were leaving a young man approached them.

'*Permiso, señorita*,' he said. 'I've seen your photo in the newspaper. You are a film-star, no?' He named a couple of films that Sharon had been in. Rick hadn't seen either.

'Yes, that's right,' Sharon said.

'I wonder if you would be so kind,' he said, taking out an address-book and a pen. 'Please.' Sharon signed her autograph. '*Muchas gracias*,' he said. 'It has been a great pleasure.'

'You're welcome,' Sharon said. The Peruvian was very polite, very formal. He smiled at Sharon, gave a curt little bow in Rick's direction, then returned to his table. Now everyone was looking towards them and whispering.

'I didn't realize you were *that* famous,' Rick said.

'I'm not,' she said. 'It must be all the publicity this film is getting in the local press.'

'Let's go then,' Rick said. 'It's only a couple of minutes' walk from here.' They left the Haiti and strolled down Avenida Ricardo Palma to Alberto's apartment. There was a light on and the sound of a Pink Floyd record issuing from his room. Rick rang the bell.

'Hi man,' Alberto said. 'Am I glad to see you!' Rick introduced Sharon. 'Wow, baby, you're beautiful,' Alberto said, then turning to Rick. 'Where did you find such a lovely girl?'

'You're high, aren't you?' Rick said superfluously.

'Since I came in from work, man. Come on in and catch me up.'

Sharon laughed at the extravagance of Alberto's compliments and while he rolled some joints told him something about herself.

'So Robert, that old entrepreneur, brought you round.'

'He's a sweet little guy,' Sharon said. 'He interviewed me for his paper and promised to introduce me to the two of you. He said you might have some dope.'

'Sure I have,' Alberto said. 'Look over here.' He opened the top drawer of his desk. It was chock-a-block with marijuana. 'Help yourself to a handful,' he said. 'I'll wrap it up for you.'

'Jean's expecting us back for dinner,' Rick said. 'She wanted to know if you'd like to come round. Afterwards we might go on to the Golden Gate or the Zanzibar.'

'Let's have a quick smoke first. I don't want to carry too much on me, especially if we're going out later.'

They smoked a couple of joints, then Alberto took a shower and put on some casual clothes to replace his office-suit. They were on the point of leaving when there was a prolonged banging on the door.

'That's weird, man,' Alberto said. 'I didn't hear the outside bell ring.' He went across to the door which was on a short chain and opened it a few inches. Rick heard him speaking in Spanish. '*Lo siento,*' he said. 'I'm sorry, but we were just going out.' There came the guttural sound of an authoritative voice. Alberto shut the door and dashed across to his desk. 'It's the fuzz,' he said. 'Get rid of those joints, Rick, and shove that grass in the garbage can, it's in the kitchen.' The knocking on the door started again.

'*Abre la puerta,*' a voice said. 'Open up.' Alberto returned and calmly opened it. Four green-uniformed, dark-skinned policemen came in. They were all armed with revolvers, holsters flapping open ominously. They took no notice of Rick or Sharon, but one of them stayed by the door. A fast and slangy conversation took place between Alberto and the officer, a Captain. Then to Rick's astonishment two of the police grabbed Alberto and pushed him roughly into a corner. Rick tried to pull one of them away.

'Keep out of it, man,' Alberto said. 'Don't be a fool. They've got a warrant.'

The policeman Rick had tackled smiled, fingering his revolver. Then they put some handcuffs on Alberto. At that moment Sharon started to cry. The Captain went over to console her.

'*Pobrecita,*' he said. 'Poor little *gringa*, she is in serious trouble, no? It is best if she pulls herself together. No harm will come to her.'

'Say nothing,' Alberto said in English. 'It seems that they followed you here. They know Sharon. They've been keeping tabs on her. There was some sort of scandal up in the sierra, but they did nothing while she was there.'

'*Callate!*' the Captain shouted. 'Speak in Spanish, *tu!*'

'I just want them to arrest me,' Alberto said. 'Then you can clear up this place. Get rid of all the stuff.'

'I said shut-up!' the Captain said and flicked out a backhander that sounded like a pistol shot across Alberto's mouth. Sharon shrieked and Rick felt his belly contract. Up to that point the episode had been almost theatrical, unreal.

'You bastard!' Rick said.

'What you say?' the Captain said. 'I spik a leetle *Inglés*, my friend. *Cuidado*.' The three others began a systematic search of Alberto's bed-sitting room. They started by sweeping all the books off the shelves, then switched to the bed.

'*No hay nada aca*,' Alberto said. 'There's nothing here.' They looked at him, smiled superciliously and went on searching. Rick found their smiles more malevolent than their anger. They were clearly enjoying themselves. The Captain had ensconced himself next to Sharon on the divan. He appeared to be talking about the film she had been making. The policeman who had been in the kitchen came back with a quantity of marijuana that Rick had dumped in the garbage can. Smiling broadly he spread a sheet of paper on the floor and dropped the grass onto it. Fastidiously the Captain picked up a bit, examined it.

'*No hay nada aca*,' he said, mimicking Alberto. 'In that case what is this?'

'It's shit, man,' Alberto said. 'We've been smoking it, yes.'

At that moment the policeman who had been methodically pulling the bed apart tipped up the mattress. There was a small bag beneath it. He picked it up, held it to the light, and dropped it in front of the Captain. He opened it and tipped some of the contents, a fine white powder, into his hand. He sniffed it cautiously.

'Ah!' he said. 'Cocaine, no?'

Alberto nodded, shrugged, then looked at Rick with an expression of weariness. 'It's cocaine,' he said flatly, 'but these two know nothing about it.'

The Captain stopped smiling, his brown face became inscrutable, his voice official. 'OK,' he said. 'We are arresting the two of you. *La señorita* may leave. We feel sure that she is completely innocent. Come, *señores, vamonos*.' They put handcuffs on Rick.

'I'm sorry,' Sharon said. 'It must be my fault.'

'It's no one's fault,' Alberto said. 'They've probably been watching me for ages.'

'Here,' Rick said. 'Take the keys of my VW. Tell Jean not to worry.'

'Come, come,' the Captain said. 'To the *comisaria*.'

Outside the night was mild. A breeze coming in from the sea carried the tang of salt. Rick noticed a jacaranda tree which was already in blossom and a knot of people standing beneath it, watching the arrest. In the police car his mind went almost completely blank for a few moments.

'Not a goddamn word,' Alberto whispered. 'You know absolutely nothing, remember? Let me do all the talking.'

They were taken to the Special Investigation Branch in San Isidro and ushered quite politely into one of the cells. It was clean and white-washed with four bunks and a couple of blankets on each. They were left for about half-an-hour. Alberto kept insisting that if questioned Rick should deny all knowledge of the drugs.

'I don't even speak Spanish,' Rick said.

'Right, man, just use English.'

'What if they know anything about the trips we made?'

'OK, we went to Guayaquil and Tarma, but you know nothing about any drugs. We were just on vacation.'

They came for Rick first. He was taken to an office where the Captain and another officer were sitting. An Indian policeman stood behind him. They took his routine details, then he was finger-printed. Afterwards they asked him for a statement.

'I don't speak Spanish well enough.'

'*Mentiroso*,' the Captain said. 'You lie. How long have you lived in Peru?'

'About four years, but I teach English, I don't have much occasion to speak Spanish.'

'Try,' the Captain said.

'OK,' Rick said. 'I called on my friend, Alberto, round about eight o'clock this evening. I was with the film actress, Sharon Winthrop. We came to invite Alberto over to my place for dinner. Then you arrived.'

'And you smoked some marijuana?'

'Alberto offered us it.'

'Look, *señor*, you are in very serious trouble. I don't know how it is in *Inglaterra*, but here it is against the law to smoke marijuana. This is not a decadent society. Here in Peru we do not approve of such vices, you understand? You are a foreigner. You are living in our country as a guest. It is a privilege we have granted you. Now all we want is a little co-operation. Things will go much more easily for you if you help us.'

'But that's all I know,' Rick said.

'Come now, my friend, is it possible? Do you take us for idiots? Do you say to yourself – this man is a stupid *cholo*, an Indian? You have been good friends, you and this Alberto Morales, you must know where he obtains his drugs. Come now, that is all we want to know. Here, have a cigarette.'

'Thanks,' Rick said, lighting the cigarette. '*Pero en verdad*, truly I don't know. I'd no idea Alberto had cocaine, if indeed it is cocaine. And, incidentally, I should like to call my Embassy before I answer any more questions.'

'Ah, you know your rights. Let me inform you, *gringo*, of the reality. Those arrested under our narcotic laws are in a special category. They have no rights. There is no *habeas corpus* for such degenerates. The military government is most anxious to eradicate such perversions. It is fundamental to the new morality.'

'Look, I'm British. I have every right to inform my Embassy if I'm arrested. You cannot hold me on circumstantial evidence.'

'In Peru you come under Peruvian law. We can hold you for interrogation as long as we wish.'

'My wife is bound to phone the Embassy.'

'They cannot help you, my friend. You can only help yourself. Tell us what you know and it might be possible to release you this evening.'

'I know nothing, I've told you.'

'All right, all right.' The policeman was suave, even affable. 'I will see you again tomorrow morning. Perhaps you will feel like talking more freely then.'

Rick was dismissed and escorted back to his cell.

'I told them nothing,' he said to Alberto. 'Just said that I wanted to contact the Embassy.'

'Good man. With luck you'll be out of her tomorrow, then you can get in touch with my solicitor and see my parents. They have influence and can help. What these shits are after is a big bribe, that's all. They don't give a damn about people smoking grass or sniffing *coke*. It's just money they want. Some goddamn bread. You should be all right though, you're British. They'll let you go tomorrow.'

Ten minutes later they came for Alberto. While he was away Rick had a visitor, Robert Redman.

'Heh, Rob,' he said. 'Is it good to see you. But how did you manage to get in?' Robert laughed, his black beard emphasising the redness of his lips.

'Well, Rick,' he said ignoring the question. 'You're in a bit of a predicament now. Sharon brought your car back. She was really shaken up. Jean too. She went round to tell Cathy what had happened. Cathy was furious. I knew it would happen sooner or later, she kept saying, it's his own fault.'

'How did you manage to get to see me?'

'You know me, I flashed my press-card and tipped them a couple of hundred, then they let me through. I've only got a few minutes though. Where's Alberto?'

'They're questioning him at the moment.'

'O.K. Now, look, Rick, the reason I came was to see if you wanted me to do anything. How much money have you got?'

'Not much.'

'Well, here's five-hundred. Pay me back later. Oh and Jean sent these cigarettes. I'm going to phone the Embassy tomorrow. Do you want me to ring Delgado at college?'

'Yes, he should be in some position to help. Besides, he'll wonder where the hell I am. He'll probably go crazy when he finds out.'

'Rick, you're a bloody idiot really, you know. I've told you to watch it with Alberto.'

'You asked me to call round on him,' Rick said. 'Anyway it was Sharon they'd been following.'

'I wouldn't be surprised if they haven't known about Alberto for

Paradise of Exiles

ages. You can't fuck around with the law in this place. The dice are loaded. You're a *gringo* and that means you're fair target.'

'That's more or less what the fuzz said to me. Implied that I'd taken advantage of their hospitality.'

'I've got to go,' Robert said. 'I'll do what I can to help and keep any report of this out of the *Herald* at least. Just one thing – don't get mad with these people, they're dangerous. Remember what happened to those convicts who escaped last year, poor bastards. Electric-shock stuff and all that. Just play it cool.'

'I'm in the untorturable class surely. I mean, I'm British. They wouldn't dare, would they?'

'Maybe not, but take it easy. Don't go blowing your top. It'll do you no good.'

'Make sure Jean's all right,' Rick said. 'I expect she's worried stiff.'

'I don't think she is,' Robert said. 'But Sheila and I will call round. Take care. See you as soon as I can.'

Robert left and one of the guards came in and asked Rick if he wanted something to eat. He did. He was starving. 'There's a Chinese restaurant across the street,' the policeman said. 'If you have money I'll go across and buy something for you.'

'No, I'll have what you've got here.'

'*No hay nada*,' said the guard. 'There's nothing.'

'All right. Get me fried rice, sweet-and-sour pork, some spring rolls and crispy noodles. Enough for my friend too.' Rick gave him the money.

'*Una cerveza tambien?*'

'You mean you can get some beer?'

'If you have enough money.'

'Get six bottles, large ones then.' The guard left. Rick lay back on his bunk smiling. It wasn't so bad, he mused, a police cell in Lima. Chinese food and beer for supper. He could put up with it for a few days.

Just then Alberto stumbled through the door and collapsed on the bunk. 'For fuck's sake,' Rick said. 'What have they done.'

'Worked me over,' Alberto said. 'I believe that's the phrase.' One of

129

his eyes was bruised and swollen. There was a cut on his lower lip and a front tooth was chipped. When he took off his shirt Rick saw that his back was covered in red welts.

'The bastards!' he said.

'They wanted to know where I got the stuff, that's all. They're not interested in us, not really. They just want the source.'

'What did you tell them?'

'Nothing till they started hitting me. Then I talked. I said I bought the grass in Guayaquil. I gave them some fictitious names and addresses. They'll never check, it's across the frontier and Peru's relations with Ecuador are never very good. I said I got the *coke* from a guy in a bar in Lima. That's when it started to get serious. They wanted to know his name, I said I didn't know . . . I'll get that bastard one day, I'll remember him, that fat pig, I'll kill him if I get out of this mess . . .'

'What did you tell them then?'

'I kept repeating my story,' Alberto said. 'Finally I described an entirely fictitious character. They'll be searching all over Lima for him now. When they can't find him, and if they realize he doesn't exist, the shit'll fly again.'

The guard came in with their Chinese meal, but neither of them felt much like eating. They drank the beer and picked at the food, then lay back smoking the cigarettes Jean had sent. After a while Alberto dropped off to sleep, exhausted.

Lying awake on that hard bunk in the narrow cell, Rick remembered when he'd first come to Lima. The city had delighted him then. He spent hours wandering around the area near Plaza de Armas with its fountain, shoeshine boys and beggars. It had the charm of the exotic in those days. He'd stroll alongside the president's palace, past the guards in their blue and red uniforms and towards the Rio Rimac, a fast-flowing turbulent stream, brown with mountain-dust, dirty with detritus. Over the bridge there was a motley collection of flat-roofed houses, churches in pink wash against the ochre hills, streets full of Indians, whole blocks of adobe houses walled in like compounds. Glimpses inside sometimes revealed little emerald lawns, orange trees, mosaic-tiled patios with tiny fountains. Beyond was the Alameda de los Descalzos with the monastery of the bare-footed monks jammed into the hillside. He'd explored it thoroughly and later shown Jean around it.

Several times he'd climbed up Cerro San Cristobal with its huge cross at the summit. He'd pass through a pink archway, along a path lined with shacks hewn out of the rock and thatched with straw. Children played by stagnant pools, dogs barked, and at the top there was a splendid view of Lima in shades of peppermint, saffron and pink. Beyond the city lay San Lorenzo Island, insubstantial, looming out of the mist coming off the Pacific. Once he had taken Jean to the church of San Francisco, twin-towered, its dome cracked like an eggshell from some earthquake. Inside they'd wandered round the catacombs where piles of white bones were heaped in pits. In one room the monks had re-assembled the skeletons of certain bishops, dressing them in tattered cowls and habits. It had made Jean shiver, especially the ghoulish spectacle of flowers fashioned from ribs and shinbones. She'd taken his hand and pressed it against her belly.

'Let's get out,' she said. 'It depresses me.' Outside she put her arm round him and clung as if physical closeness was an antidote. And indeed it was, he thought. Warm flesh, the contact of bodies. Now in this cell he longed for the reassurance of Jean's touch, her tenderness.

He woke at dawn with grey light filtering through the bars. He felt cold. With a sinking sensation he remembered where he was. He looked at Alberto. They'd certainly made a mess of his face. Rick's mouth tasted rotten. He wanted a shower, but there were no facilities. Alberto was morose and silent. He kept touching the bruise round his eye. A guard came in with some weak coffee. Afterwards they were escorted to the lavatory and allowed to wash in cold water. Back in the cell they began a game of poker with a deck of cards the guard had lent them.

Two hours later Rick was taken away for further questioning.

'Say whatever comes into your head,' Alberto advised. 'Give them all the information they want. Invent it. If they start anything, scream the word – embassy – and go on screaming it.'

Rick was taken to a different office. It was whitewashed and bare except for a desk and some notices on the wall. The same Captain, his brown face phlegmatic, his heavy body paunchy in green uniform, was sitting back in his chair. He smiled, or rather sneered at Rick whose belly fluttered momentarily as he glanced into his small dark eyes. His legs felt rubbery and weak. So this was what it had come to, he thought, this sojourn in a foreign country – a square white room and an Indian policeman who was probably a sadist of some sort.

'*Buenos dias,*' the Captain said with what Rick regarded as a feigned cordiality. 'I hope this morning you are going to be more helpful.'

'I should like to contact the British Embassy,' Rick said.

'Hah, you are a little frightened, I can see. A little yellow streak begins to show now. You didn't appreciate the sight of your friend's injuries, eh?'

'You can't touch me,' Rick said. 'There would probably be an enquiry.'

The Captain laughed. 'You have a big opinion of your own importance. Let me tell you, you are nothing. *Nada.* Your British Embassy will not care. A drug addict! That is something to be proud of, no?' He got up abruptly and came towards Rick. The guard with whom he'd been playing poker flinched uneasily. Rick could smell chili on the Captain's breath. When he spoke a fine spittle sprayed his cheek. 'We're ready to release you,' the Captain said. 'You are of no importance. You are nothing to us. A shit. A fuck-up. A foreigner who smokes marijuana. Pff! *Nada.* A *gringo* with a big opinion of himself and no balls. Who trembles when I, *un pobre serrano*, a poor Indian from Cuzco speaks. All right, *está bien*, we don't want you. You can go today. This minute. *Este dia hoy*, if you tell us the truth. Tell us where your dear friend obtains this marijuana and this illegal white powder, this cocaine. That's all.'

'I've told you, I've no idea, I don't know. I never ask Alberto. I don't want to know.'

'They are very close, these two, no?' he said to the guard. 'This gringo and his Peruvian friend. Perhaps they are fairies, no?' The guard smiled in automatic response. 'These *maricónes*, they often use drugs, it is part of their general depravity, no? But they are *cobardes*, all of them. Cowards.'

'If you think I'm frightened of you, or any of the Peruvian police, you must be joking,' Rick said.

The Captain's face showed no expression, a brown mask, then it cracked into a partial smile. 'What bravado,' he said, then turning to the guard. 'The *gringo* says he's not a coward, but I say he's a *maricón*, a fairy. A pervert.' He turned back to Rick and without warning punched him in the solar plexus. It was so sudden he scarcely felt any pain, only shock, his breath gone. As he bent over, gasping, the Captain's khaki-green knee whipped into his face. Rick felt the rough serge of the cloth, the pain shooting along a nerve into his head. Tears came involuntarily into his eyes. He tried to hold them, wondering whether his jaw-bone had been fractured.

'Fuck you!' he muttered in English and feebly attempted to take a swing at the Captain, but the guard grabbed his arms. '*Hijo de puta*,' he added in Spanish.

'So, so,' the Captain said. 'You insult me, no? You insult my Indian heritage. Then you hit me or try to.' He stepped close to Rick and slapped him three or four times with the back of his hand, each blow felt to Rick as if it had drawn blood. His face felt burning, puffy. 'OK, so now you will talk. Now you will tell us the truth or there will be more games.'

'I don't know anything.'

The Captain picked up a black truncheon that was lying on his desk. Rick ducked his head in anticipation of the blow, then yelled as the Captain struck his knee-caps with it. The pain was intense and if he had not been held he would have collapsed.

'Release him,' the Captain said and Rick dropped to the floor. He sat there until the guard pulled him to his feet. Christ, he'd done nothing but play the part of a hero since his return to Peru, he thought, but beneath it all he *was* a coward. He was shit scared. This Indian bastard could see through him all right. He'd seen that Rick was yellow. The Captain fingered the truncheon again.

'We got it from Ecuador,' Rick almost shouted. 'I don't know who from, Alberto does. We got the marijuana from Guayaquil. We went up by car some time ago. I don't know about the cocaine, I really don't, please believe me, I swear it's true!'

'Good boy,' the Captain said. 'Come, sit down here. Now you are beginning to help us. That's good, *bueno*. Now I want you to make another statement and sign it, OK? Begin with what you have just told me. I want to know everything. How long you were in Guayaquil and where you stayed. How you got the stuff across the frontier and also what you were doing in Tarma recently.'

It took Rick half-an-hour to fill out the statement, inventing the details and disguising the facts as much as possible. When it was signed and completed the Captain gave him a cigarette.

'What's going to happen now?' Rick said.

'Who knows?' the Captain said. 'We're holding you for the moment, of course. Perhaps your Embassy will help, I don't know. There are plenty of things to clear up first. I want to check the facts that you have given us. And I'll need to question you again. Tomorrow, perhaps.'

Back in the cell Rick lay down on his bunk. He had never felt so powerless, nor so humiliated in his life. He could have broken down and wept, surrendering completely to the weakness that had come over him.

'Did they mess you about?' Alberto said.

'I lost my temper.'

'What did you tell them?'

'Pretty well everything, but I made up a lot of the facts.'

'That's OK, I did the same. They're putting me in the central prison, El Sexto. I'm being charged, but it's all got to be presented before a judge. A preliminary hearing, it's called. I don't know what they're doing about you.'

'At the moment I don't particularly care.'

'Listen, Rick, do you want to smoke a joint?'

'Here? You must be joking.'

'No, man, I bought it from the guy on guard. He's probably got hold of some of *my* marijuana.'

'That's crazy.'

'Like I told you,' Alberto said. 'It's all corrupt. It's just the bread they're after. They don't give a sweet goddamn about anything else.'

Paradise of Exiles

They sat back, leaning against the white-washed wall while Alberto rolled a joint, lit it, then handed it to Rick. Within ten minutes they were chuckling together.

'Tonight, we'll have steak and chips for supper,' Alberto said. 'And a couple of bottles of wine. I've already fixed it with our friend.'

'It's crazy,' Rick said, 'this Peruvian system.'

Jean bathed the children, tucked them up in bed and began to read a story to the girls before they went to sleep.

'Where's Daddy?' Sara said, interrupting her.

'He's had to go away for a few days,' Jean said. 'He'll be back soon.'

'He didn't tell us he was going,' Sara said.

'He had to go on a trip into the mountains,' Jean said. 'But don't worry, he'll be home soon.'

She finished reading the story, kissed them goodnight, then went into the kitchen to see how the dinner was coming along.

'Why did he have to go?' Sara shouted after her.

'He had a job to do,' Jean said. 'Now off to sleep, all of you.'

She glanced at the saucepan. It was simmering gently and an aroma of herbs wafted through the flat. Cathy, Robert and Sheila were coming round to discuss what could be done about Rick and Alberto. Jean was making an Italian dish of tripe, onions and tomatoes, with rice. Preparing the meal took her mind off her immediate concerns, but didn't allay her anxiety.

At one time Lima had been such a good place to live that she'd actually longed to return. She must have been seeing it then through rose-tinted glasses, because surely it wasn't the city that had changed but her attitude to it. Rick had criticised it, but his outbursts had undoubtedly been sparked off by personal experience. And when he had wanted to fly back to England she'd persuaded him to stick it out. Things would improve, she'd said, and indeed they had until this last foolish incident. For a moment she wondered what would happen if Rick were to get a prison sentence. Doctor Delgado would never go on paying a salary to a teacher who was in prison. She would be on her own. There would be no alternative but to leave. The Embassy would probably have to repatriate her.

135

She fixed the potato salad and avocados they were having for starters, poured herself a *pisco*, topping it up with ice-cold Coca Cola, and took it into the sitting-room. She put on the Beatles' *Here comes the sun*, which always cheered her up. As she straightened up from the record-player she felt a familiar spasm of pain in her shoulder. It forced her to lean against the wall for support. It was exactly like the one she'd had on the afternoon of the earthquake. She was sure it was cancer, the cells rioting in her body. And yet she was only thirty-five. Surely people didn't get it that young. She smoked quite a lot, but then so did hundreds of their friends. Once Rick was back home she would have to go to the doctor's. Perhaps it was just a touch of asthma, she thought, sinking down on the divan, half-expecting the pain to re-occur.

She'd had asthma twice before, the first time just after Sara was born. It was a difficult birth. She was heavily sedated in the hospital and the doctor there had explained that the asthma was probably a combination of the drugs and anxiety. It disappeared quickly and then she had been more worried about being constipated because her stitches had hurt so much. She'd forgotten both in her vaguely-astonished rapture over Sara. Her second asthmatic attack had come a long time afterwards when she'd been smoking some of Alberto's marijuana. Rick had given her quantities of black coffee on that occasion and in between spasms of difficult breathing she'd even been laughing.

The doorbell rang. It was Cathy and Robert.

'Sheila couldn't make it,' Robert said. 'I think she's picked up the flu.'

'That's all right,' Jean said.

'I've brought a bottle of wine,' Cathy said.

'The dinner's all ready. I just have to serve it. Robert, why don't you fix us some drinks?'

Robert made *pisco* sours while Jean brought the meal out on a tray and they sat round the low table in the lounge, helping themselves. Robert replaced *Abbey Road* with some Brubeck jazz. Jean listened to the others talk. The room with its turquoise divan and red easy-chairs, Japanese prints and an abstract based on a cock-fight on the walls, the bookshelves full of books, was warm and cosy, especially after a couple of drinks. The cold realities were outside, beyond the white walls of the flat. For her it was an island of security. When she went onto the patio that led off the kitchen, having cleared away their plates, she could see the lights of the city, their reddish glow, the strip of ocean at Miraflores with San Lorenzo island still outlined against the afterglow of sunset.

'What's the news then?' she asked on her return, having delayed the question throughout the meal.

'I was at the Embassy this morning,' Robert said. 'They don't want to interfere, not at the moment.'

'They've got to do something.'

'They're going to send someone round to make a few routine enquiries.'

'They should make a fuss.'

'I think Rick'll be out soon whatever the Embassy do. They can't hold him indefinitely, not a British subject.'

'Alberto's solicitor told me they're holding him,' Cath said. 'He'll be charged with possession. I've seen his parents and his father's going to find out who the judge is for the preliminary hearing. It's becoming a question of bribes and politics as far as I can see. Family influence and all that. It'll probably cost them a small fortune.'

'You can get away with murder if you know the right people,' Robert said.

'When are you and Sheila off to the States?' Cath asked.

'As soon as my documents come through. It'll be a month or so yet.'

'I hope to be gone in the New Year,' Cath said. 'I've begun to apply for posts.'

'That'll only leave Rick, myself and Alberto,' Jean said. 'That is if they're released.'

'If not, come to the States with me,' Cath said smiling.

'Or with Sheila and me,' Robert said.

'I might have to. Doctor Delgado was round today. He was doing his nut. Kept on about the bad publicity for the college if it's discovered that one of his teachers has been arrested on a narcotics charge.'

'It'll make Rick a hero with those teenage students of his,' Cath said. 'But that Delgado is just an old hypocrite.'

137

'I told him to do something to help if he felt like that. Use his influence.'

'What happened to that American girl, Sharon?'

'I only saw her once after that evening,' Robert said. 'She got out in a hurry. It really upset her, the whole business.'

'That'll be a disappointment for Rick,' Jean said. 'I think he fancied her.'

'From what I heard they all did,' Cath said.

'Well, she was attractive,' Robert said.

'I preferred her bloke, Pierre,' Jean said. 'Now I could have quite taken to him.'

'I suppose you know that Sharon has been in several films.'

'I'm not impressed, if that's what you mean. I thought she was quite incredibly naive.'

'That's just her Californian manner,' Cath said. 'She's probably sharp as a razor beneath that innocent surface.'

'I wish you hadn't brought her round that evening,' Jean said. 'I know she's not really responsible, but none of this would have happened otherwise.'

'It'll be a salutary lesson for them both,' Cathy said. 'I know that sounds hard, but I've been warning Alberto for ages. I just hope he'll be more sensible once he's out.'

They finished the wine, then went on to the *pisco* while Robert played Rick's jazz records. About midnight Cath decided to leave. She was teaching in the morning and wanted a reasonably early night.

'Stay for a coffee,' Jean said.

'No, I really must get back.'

'I'd like one if that's all right,' Robert said.

After Cath had left, Jean went into the kitchen to make the coffee. Somehow she didn't want to be alone, to brood over Rick or the pain in her shoulder. She waited for the coffee to boil, then took it into the lounge on a tray. Robert had put on a Stan Getz that was quiet and soothing. Glancing at him for a moment, Jean recalled the time they'd made love. She could remember his smooth suntanned body and the silky feel of his beard. It had been pleasant that night, not so exciting as it sometimes was with Rick, but enjoyable enough. Now she didn't really want to face that desert of a double-bed alone. The thought of doing so for days, even weeks perhaps, depressed her. She wanted the warmth and comfort of physical contact, Rick would have understood that surely.

'Have you got to go soon?' Jean asked. 'Will Sheila be waiting up for you?'

He looked at her a little quizzically and Jean wasn't sure that he had understood. That was one of the difficulties. A woman had to be more tactful and oblique than a man. Though surely she could be open with Robert. They'd known each other long enough, but a rejection could hurt and she didn't want to risk one. It would only make her feel worse.

'She's really not well,' Robert said. 'I imagine she'll be asleep now, but I don't want to leave her alone too long.' He smiled again, a little sheepishly, Jean thought, as if somehow she had called his bluff.

'All right,' she said. 'I won't keep you. It's just that I'm trying to stave off depression.'

'Of course, I'll stay a while longer,' he said. 'You know I've always loved you,' he added laughing lightly.

'Don't say things like that,' she said. 'You don't have to and they're not true anyway. I'm lonely and fed up, that's all.'

'I'll never understand women,' he said. 'No matter how much I try.'

'Don't try,' she said. 'Do you think any man does? It's even a little presumptuous to try.'

He laughed, but wryly, as if he'd been caught out saying something insensitive or even stupid. He wanted to leave. He regretted his promise to have another coffee.

'I'm afraid I'll have to go soon,' he said.

'I know,' she said. 'Don't worry, I'll let you leave.' She was laughing quietly to herself. Robert smiled. They talked for a while longer, but Jean herself was beginning to feel drowsy. She knew she would sleep all right that night. As Robert was about to go he held her and kissed her on the cheek.

'I'll do what I can about the Embassy,' he said. 'Now look after yourself and we'll call round in a day or two. Sooner if there's any definite news.'

139

'Goodnight, Robert,' she said. 'Thanks for coming. I'll see you both soon.'

'Take care,' he said.

She heard the door downstairs slam to, then a car engine revving up outside on the apartment-block. On an impulse she checked the children. The three of them were sleeping soundly. And a few minutes after getting into bed she too was asleep.

Through the intervention of the Embassy Rick was released three days later. He had not been questioned again, but was advised to leave the country within three months. Back at college Doctor Delgado told him that he would be obliged to terminate his contract at the end of the academic year. Rick protested about this, but secretly he was delighted.

'I'll pay you for the holidays,' Delgado said. 'Plus the two extra months of salary for the two years you've taught here and I'll pay your own fare back to London. I hope there are no hard feelings. We've enjoyed having you here, but I can't take chances with the military government. They're still talking about nationalising the private colleges.'

'I understand,' Rick said.

That afternoon he went into Lima and booked their passage back to Europe on an Italian boat. They were to leave on New Year's Eve. He was able to pay the fares for Jean and the children by selling his red VW. Within three months they would be leaving. With a three-week cruise to look forward to. Even arrest and trouble with the authorities had its compensations. That night he and Jean went out to dinner to celebrate.

At the Institute he met with another cool reception. His services as a lecturer were no longer required. Rick had put them in a very delicate position, the director said. The students, clearly disappointed, arranged for Rick to give his remaining lectures privately. Ironically, they offered to pay him more than the Institute had done.

Alberto was finally released three weeks after Rick himself. He came out of prison looking much thinner and paler. He was run down and had developed a nervous tic of the right eyelid. He and Rick went for a drink to celebrate.

'They withdrew the charges, man,' Alberto said. 'Insufficient evidence.'

'What about the *coke* they found and the grass in the garbage can?'

'It seems to have disappeared. The police must have got rid of it. Lack of evidence. That was the official verdict.'

'It's laughable.'

'Not for my parents. I'm afraid. It cost them about two-thousand dollars. Various police officials got half of that and the judge who heard the case, an old acquaintance of my father's, got the rest.'

'And the military go on about their new morality.'

'All bull, man, to impress the people. You can't change a country overnight. Everyone's out for what he can get. Judges, the police, the lot. I almost feel sorry for the military. They're up against centuries of corruption. A pirateering tradition. It goes back to the *conqistadores*.'

'I come to get gold not to till the soil like a peasant.'

'Yeh, well, it's still the same. Except the present conquerors are those guys with sinecures in the bureaucracy, landowners and foreign capitalists. If the military can do something to change it, I'm all for it. It really needs a Marxist take-over.'

'You sound like Julio Scorza.'

'Well, he's right.'

'I suppose so. After my interview with that Captain, I reckon if I were Peruvian I'd be prepared to fight for it. Run off to the jungle as a guerrilla.'

'The revolution needs to start in the city,' Alberto said. 'Here in Lima. It needs a movement like the *Tupamaros* – urban guerrillas.'

'Your attitudes have certainly changed.'

'Man, if there's any place designed to convert an easy-going middle-class bum into a revolutionary, it's El Sexto.'

'What was it like?'

'A goddamn hell on earth. It's the worst three weeks I've ever spent. The stench when you first go in nearly makes you faint. Over a thousand men in a place built for two hundred. Not enough lavatories. You have to queue for everything, even a crap. At the end of the day the ablution area is swilling in piss. I was in a cell for three with seven other guys.'

'Oddly enough' he said, 'there's a fair amount of freedom of a sort. There are too many prisoners to look after. You can wander around except that the corridors are full of jostling men. The place is really run by the prisoners and you can get anything for money – if you have enough. But you're screwed without it. You can get cigs, books, food, and even rent a TV if you've got the bread. If you haven't you could easily starve. The food's just slop. I sent out for everything I ate. The guards make a pile out of it.'

'Was there much violence?'

'I steered clear of it, but there are outbreaks all the time. The worst thing is the discomfort though. If you've got no money, you can't even get medical treatment. The place is full of TB, clap and enteritis. So I was told.'

'What were the other prisoners like?'

'Convicted criminals, those awaiting trial, political prisoners – everyone's together. You can wait up to two years for a trial, get sentenced to six months and find you've served four times that already. No recompense. It's just your bad luck. On the other hand you can bribe the guards to let you out for a few hours to see your wife or girlfriend.'

'What if you tried to escape?'

'You'd be a dead duck, man, if they caught up with you . . . But come on, let's smoke some grass down at the sea-front before we have any more beer.'

'You're not serious, are you?'

'Sure,' Alberto said smiling. 'So long as we keep clear of your place and mine, we'll be OK.'

Jean sat on the black poncho by the edge of the stream and laid out lunch on cardboard plates. There was cold chicken, avocado and salad. She buttered bread rolls and poured out cups of Coca Cola. The sun was burning on her face. Below her David was playing in the white dust near the water's edge. His hair was almost white in the sunlight. Near him, Emma, wearing a T-shirt to keep the sun off her body, paddled in the stream that gurgled over pebbles yellowed with algae. Among the thorn trees and clumps of bamboo, green in contrast to

Paradise of Exiles

the grey mountains beyond, Rick and Sara were searching for ant-lions. Under the eucalyptus trees, near the parked cars, two donkeys were grazing. Their occasional hawing, a melancholy sound, made her glance up from time to time.

She finished laying out lunch and shouted to the others. Rick collected Emma from the stream and with Sara tagging behind came up to the poncho. Jean strolled over to David, picked him up with an arm around his middle and carried him over. The girls had started to eat. After lunch the adults sat in the shade of some tall ferns talking desultorily and smoking cigarettes. Jean watched the blue wreaths of smoke curling up, strange in the clear light before vanishing in the warm air.

'It's beautiful up here,' she said.

'Yes, I like it.'

'The quiet and emptiness,' she said. 'I feel it's our place.'

'There are a couple of cars including an Alfa Romeo parked in the shade of those trees,' Rick said.

'I know, but there's so much space, you don't even meet anyone else.'

'And further up,' Rick said, 'I saw a Scout camp, some lads out for the weekend. Look, you can see the red and white flag between the ferns.'

'I'm going to take the kids down to the stream for a swim,' Jean said.

'Think I'll sunbathe for a bit.'

She walked down to the water's edge followed by the children. They pushed their way through the underbrush to a white boulder. In the pool formed by the partial damming of the water's flow there was a shoal of fish that looked like stickleback. Jean broke up a piece of bread one of the children had left and threw it in. The fish attacked the crumbs with the voracity of miniature sharks. Sitting beside the pool the children watched, fascinated. Suddenly Sara, who was naked, jumped into the stream, the fish scattered and a sandy sediment clouded the water. Sara jumped up and down stirring up more mud and Emma, her hair like burnished copper, joined her.

'You've frightened the fish away,' Jean said. The girls laughed and

David struggled in her arms, anxious to leap into the water too. Near the grove where they'd eaten Jean noticed a couple of stray dogs foraging for scraps. She wondered where Rick had got to, then saw him perched high up on a huge boulder above the greenery. He was gazing up the valley to where the hills seemed to merge in haze. His hair was long and brown with chestnut tints in the sun, she noted, his regular profile a bit solemn, as if his thoughts were miles away, lost in some dream or regret, some ambition or disappointment, she wasn't sure which. He'd been quieter, less restless, more attentive and content since the episode in the Lima jail. It had probably shaken him, she thought, and had to suppress a smile. Anyway he now seemed determined to take it easy until the end of the year when they were due to leave.

'Rick, come and look after the kids for a while,' she shouted. 'I'd like to go for a walk.'

He jumped down from the boulder, an athletic litheness about his movement, came crashing through some brush, and joined her. 'OK,' he said. 'There are some old ruins a few hundred yards away up the slope. You should go and have a look at them.'

She left him entertaining the children and scrambled up the path until she emerged on the scree slope. She was quite breathless and felt a twinge of familiar pain in her shoulder. For a few hours she'd forgotten all about it, but, striking now, it brought back the fear which she was also growing accustomed to. The worst thing was not knowing what its cause was, though the idea of going to the doctor's scared her more. It might only be a touch of asthma or a side effect of the bronchitis she'd had on and off for six months now. But she would wait until they were back in England before having a thorough check-up.

Having recovered her breath Jean climbed further up the scree. Below her she could see Rick bending over the stream, the children all crouched beside him. They were probably watching the stickleback again, but the sight of them together left her with a feeling of sadness. The thought that something might happen to any of them, or to herself; the sudden thought that she might not see the children grow up, the two girls becoming more like her all the time, growing close like sisters, Rick with David more as time went on, teaching him to play football and cricket; the very thought that anything should interrupt the progress of family life, their domestic contentment, terrified her.

She clambered laboriously to the summit of the scree. The sun was extremely hot, the light brilliant so that the mauve shadows of ridges and indentations in the rock, the little hollows and bumps of the foothills, were clearly defined and the silvery-green leaves of the eucalyptus trees shimmered in the heat. She sat down on an overhang of rock, saw a fat yellow-and-black spider at the centre of its web stretching from some bracken and almost at eye-level. A lizard shot past her through the dust. And above the jagged line of hills was a faint crescent moon almost invisible against the blueness of the sky.

She rested for several minutes, then moved on to the ruins, a mass of rubble, shale and sunbaked adobe. She lingered among the tumbled stones, finding some white and chalky bone, fragile as a fossil, brittle and crumbling into dust. Then between some rocks, a skull, four-hundred years old perhaps, with a piece of reddish hair that must have once been black, still adhering to it. It was coarse to the touch like the mane of a horse. Despite the heat she shuddered and began to make her way back to the stream.

'Did you see the ruins?' Rick asked.

'Yes, there are some old bones up there.'

'I know,' he said. 'Most of these small Incaic ruins have never been excavated. Too many of them.'

'I expect anything of value has gone.'

'You might find something if you really searched.'

'It gave me the creeps,' she said.

'It is a bit macabre, I know.'

They collected their stuff, gathered the kids and walked over to the car which Cathy had lent them for the day. The metal roof was too hot to touch. They scrambled in, Rick put it into second and they drove up the track, looping round until they came to a point where it narrowed and a fall of loose rock blocked the way. Rick did a three-point turn and they bounced back down, moving more quickly as they descended. Once in the narrow stretch of plain, purple and gold with flowering shrubs, Rick speeded up.

'I'd like to get back reasonably early,' he said. 'I've got some notes on Byron to finish and I'd like to work on those new Scorza poems later. Would you help me get them finished?'

'Yes, I'd like that.'

It had been one of those good days, she thought, as Rick began the climb along the metal road through the pass. She'd felt good from the moment she'd woken up that morning and realized that summer had almost arrived. Even on the coast there was a gleam of blue sky and the buildings looked whiter, the plazas greener, rooftops festive with washing, and kites had been circling. From the balcony she'd caught sight of the sea's glitter and had decided at that moment on a picnic in the hills. It had been the sort of day she could hoard in memory, to hold against the weekly routine, the disagreements with Rick, the pain in her shoulder.

Rick changed down into second, passed a dawdling car on the curve of the pass – which always reminded Jean of some gulch set for an ambush in a Western; then they began to accelerate through low hills into the mist and suburbs, the pale glint of the Pacific about ten kilometres in front of them. The kids were chatting in the back seat. And Jean was looking forward to a steaming mug of black coffee and some cakes for tea.

Chapter Ten

At the end of October Rick gave the first of his lectures on Byron. It was held in a Spanish-style villa in the luxury suburb of Montericco. Irma, friendlier than she'd been the last time he'd seen her, took him there in her blue sports-car and introduced him to the assembled women. After the introductions he began. He went over the salient incidents in Byron's life, quoted from his letters, then read a few passages from *Childe Harold*. Finally, he came to *Don Juan*, reading the first few verses, then dipping into the opening *Cantos* to illustrate Byron's irony and wit. When he finished they applauded. There was wine to follow and a cheque for fifty dollars. Afterwards Irma drove him back to Miraflores, smiling to herself as they sped down the highway into the city.

'You are a bit of a bastard,' she said eventually with a grin.

'How do you mean?'

'Exploiting those women like that.'

'Like what?'

'You try to appear so cynical, so Byronic yourself,' she said. 'And now they'll all go home dissatisfied, imagining they understand Byron's poetry, a bit in love with him. Or a bit in love with you.'

'That's ridiculous,' he said. 'I was merely giving a lecture, I don't know what you're trying to say.'

'You try to impress, that's what I mean,' she said. 'By attitudinising.'

'I wish you were a bit more impressed.'

'How do you know I'm not?'

'Not enough to go to that motel with me,' he said. 'I've had a bad time the last few months, it's a wonder I'm still sane.'

'You poor thing!' Irma said laughing lightly. 'My heart bleeds for you. Like your hero, Byron, you've got everything mixed up. *They* might be convinced, but I'm not, not in the least.' She stopped at the far corner of the plaza, waited until he'd got out, then gave him a tantalising smile. 'See you next week,' she said and accelerated away.

He strolled across the yellowed grass, dodging some kids who were playing football. Irma seemed to have a completely false idea of what he was like. He didn't deliberately try to project an image. It was true that he could be amused by Byron's ironies, but they had little to do with his feelings towards Jean or the children. And for that matter nothing to do with the fear he'd felt in the hands of the police. It was all very well to play at being the hero, but that was nothing much more than a game, a pretence of courage. In reality he was weak enough – and that police captain had seen right through him.

In front of their apartment block he met Jean who was loaded down with bags of groceries. Behind her tagged Sara and Emma.

'Give me those bags,' Rick said. 'Have you walked all the way from the supermarket?'

'It's all right,' she said. 'Cathy's coming round later to bring a copy of the anthology. We must celebrate that.'

'I'd forgotten,' he said. 'Heh, what's the matter? You look as if you've been crying.'

'I had a row with that flower-seller, you know the one I mean, who always pesters you until you buy something. He gave me the evil-eye, I mean he really did, because I got annoyed and wouldn't buy any flowers.'

'The evil-eye?'

'He cursed me. I know it's a load of superstitious mumbo-jumbo, but it upset me, I'm afraid.'

'Where is he now?'

'Leave it, Rick, it was nothing really. He just came out with this stream of abuse, wishing upon me a variety of unpleasant things.'

'That's him over there, isn't it?'

'Yes, but leave it and come and tell me how the lecture went down.'

'In a minute,' he said and sprinted across the plaza to where the flower-seller was still standing. 'What did you say to my wife?' he said in Spanish. 'I'd like an explanation.'

Paradise of Exiles

'*Señor?*' He was thin and delicate-looking, the flower-seller, with a shrewd and shifty expression, but the melancholy eyes of so many Indians. '*Señor*, I don't understand. I know your *señora*, she often buys flowers from me. Why should I annoy her?'

'She was in tears.'

'I am sorry, *señor*, but I do not understand. I said nothing to upset her.'

'Ah fuck it!' Rick said and walked away. It wasn't possible to pick a fight with someone who was so apologetic. The poor sod probably had to take all sorts of shit from the people in that district. Possibly he hadn't sold any flowers all day and would have to take more shit from his family when he got home at night.

'He denied it,' Rick said to Jean.

'Of course he would. Let's just forget the incident.'

They went up in the lift, had some coffee, then Rick bathed the kids while Jean prepared dinner. When Cathy arrived the children were tucked up in bed asleep, the drinks were on the table and the meal almost ready. In her excitement at seeing their book of Peruvian poetry in translation Jean appeared to have forgotten the dispute with the flower-seller.

'It's certainly elegant looking,' she said. 'Have you checked it through yet?'

'I was so thrilled getting it, I wanted to start on more translations straight away,' Cath said. 'We should get some individual collections out. I've brought these drafts of the new Julio Scorza poems and wondered whether we could check them through before we eat.'

'What about a drink first?'

'Well, just one until we've finished.'

Rick mixed rum-and-cokes, took one to Jean in the kitchen, then poured himself a beer. He lit a cigarette and for the next hour went over the translations Cathy had brought with her.

'I'm having a Halloween party for the kids tomorrow,' Jean said when she brought in the meal. 'Why don't you bring yours round too?' She showed Cathy the pumpkin she had hollowed out. 'I'm going to put candles inside.'

149

'Of course I'll come, Cathy said, 'The kids will love it. Is there anything you'd like me to bring?'

'I'm going to make sandwiches, get some crisps, biscuits, cake and icecream. You could bring something to drink if you like.'

'Some Coca Cola and orange juice?'

'That sounds fine.'

'Let's have another drink ourselves,' Rick said.

'Open the wine,' Jean said.

For dinner she had prepared prawn cocktails and avocados to start with, chicken Maryland for the main course, mango and papaya for dessert. After they'd finished the wine, Jean and Cathy had several more rum-and-cokes while Rick finished the beer. They spent the rest of the evening discussing their plans. With the book now out, Cathy was hopeful of obtaining a teaching post in the States, Rick was excited by the prospect of finding publishers for individual selections once he was back in England, and Jean was looking forward to a lazy voyage home in an Italian ship at the end of December.

Just after midnight Cathy decided to leave. 'I'll see you tomorrow then, Jean. I'm sure the kids will be delighted.'

'Think I'll go to the beach,' Rick said. 'Keep out of your way.'

'Why not?' Cath said. 'Jean and I can manage all right.'

'I thought you might like to help.'

'Well, if you want me to, of course I will.' Cathy left and Jean went in to check on the children. They were sleeping soundly. She and Rick went to bed themselves and still slightly high from the wine they made love. Afterwards they shared a cigarette and then Rick dropped off to sleep.

It was about four o'clock when Jean woke him up. She was sitting up in bed, sweat pouring down her face and trickling between her breasts, her breathing rapid and hoarse, the bedside lamp turned on. She coughed and the sound was harsh, rasping. 'Rick,' she said between coughs, 'would you get me some of that cough-syrup we bought for the children? I think it's in the kitchen.'

'Are you all right?' Rick said. 'That cough sounds bad. I think you should see a doctor about it.'

Paradise of Exiles

'I will in the morning. I've got this pain in my shoulder and my breathing feels constricted.'

He went to the kitchen and found the medicine. He poured out a table-spoonful and gave it to Jean. She swallowed it and coughed. A rasping noise was still issuing from her throat. She looked very pale, her face drawn, a little haggard even.

'Do you want me to call the doctor now?' he said. 'I can phone from the Italians' apartment opposite.'

'No, I'll make an appointment to see him tomorrow.'

'Are you sure you're all right?'

'I think I'm going to be sick.'

He dashed into the children's playroom where their son was sleeping and grabbed one of the beach-buckets. When he came back Jean was sitting up on the edge of the bed. He held the bucket for her as she retched and vomited into it. Her vomit was thin. It looked like a mixture of phlegm and cough syrup, dark brown and viscous. 'I think I should get a doctor now,' he said.

'No, please don't, I'm feeling better now,' Jean said. 'The pain is easing off a bit.' She lay back, her head on the pillow. Rick looked at her carefully. She seemed better and her breathing was less harsh.

'That cough has persisted for months,' he said. 'I think you ought to try and stop smoking. Cut it down at least.' Jean didn't answer. She was apparently asleep, her face still pale, but her breathing almost normal. Rick got back into bed beside her. Outside it was still dark and almost at once he fell into a light sleep.

It was dawn when he woke up again, a grey light filtering through the slats in the Persian blinds. Jean was sitting up in bed, her breathing coming in short gasps, her eyes staring unnaturally. She was totally pre-occupied, her strength concentrated on trying to regulate her breathing. Shocked, Rick turned to her, grabbing her by the shoulders.

'Jean, for Christ's sake!' he said. Her shoulders were cold with damp sweat and her breathing sounded peculiar as if she were having an asthmatic attack.

'Jean, Jean!' he said, shaking her, trying to provoke a reaction. Close to panic he got out of bed.

'Jesus Christ!' he muttered. 'Shit!' He put on his trousers, looked

151

round at his wife. 'Jean,' he said. Her breathing seemed to be worsening. He dashed out of the room and across to the Italians' flat opposite. He rang the bell, but no one answered. He waited, ringing continuously. Still no one came to the door. He ran down the first flight of steps to the flat below and rang it. A neighbour, Señora Vargas, opened the door. She was in her dressing-gown.

'My wife is ill,' Rick said, his Spanish confused in the panic. 'Please can you phone the doctor. Tell him it's an emergency.' There was a further delay as Señora Vargas brought the telephone-directory and gave it to Rick who looked up the number. He rushed back upstairs. Their Italian neighbours had woken up and were standing at their door.

'My wife's ill,' he said.

Hoarse gasps of breath were coming from Jean's open mouth. Her head had dropped back on the pillow and was turned towards the open window. Sara, their daughter, who had woken up, was standing by the side of the bed, gazing at her mother. Her face was pale and solemn.

'Sit up!' Rick shouted. 'Jean, sit up!' He had never heard such a sound before. Her breathing was alien, almost like a spasmodic bark. He tried to make her sit up, his arm round her shoulders. She half-raised her head, her eyes wide, an expression of surprise on her face, her breathing like an irregular hacksaw. Then she collapsed back on the pillow. Rick ran downstairs again and begged Señora Vargas to get her car out. They hadn't got time to wait for the doctor; Jean was too sick. Señora Vargas followed him upstairs. He ran up, three steps at a time, heard the sound of Jean's breathing, saw Sara still standing there.

'Go back to your room' he said. 'Mummy's sick.'

He leaned over Jean. 'Sit up, please,' he said. He had the idea that movement would help her. But abruptly, as he was bent over her, Jean's breathing stopped and her jaw dropped open with a strange exhalation. Rick shook her by the shoulders, but her body dropped back, heavy and slack. He couldn't believe it. It couldn't be true. Scarcely ten minutes had elapsed since he had woken the second time.

Paradise of Exiles

He had to get her to hospital. She needed oxygen to revive her. At that moment Señora Vargas appeared in the doorway. She took a quick look at Jean and shrieked.

'*Madre de Dios*,' she said. '*Madre de Dios!*' And began to sob.

'Help me get her downstairs,' Rick said.

Together they lifted her, wrapped a dressing-gown around her and managed, half-dragging her legs, to get to the lift, then across the carpark to the Señora's VW. Rick propped her up in the backseat, her weight against him. As Señora Vargas drove off Jean emitted a sort of gasp. She was alive then. They just had to hurry. Ten minutes later they were outside the American Clinic and attendants carried her inside on a stretcher.

'*Está muerta*,' the nurse said after taking one quick glance at the body. Rick wasn't sure he had heard the Spanish correctly. A doctor was called and the trolley upon which she lay was pushed behind some curtained-off cubicle. A few minutes later the doctor came over to Rick.

'Your wife is dead,' he said. 'She was dead on arrival, I'm afraid, and the Clinic cannot accept responsibility. I shall have the body taken to the chapel, then we'll have to phone for the Police. I'm sorry, señor, but they have to be informed.'

Rick sat in the waiting-room, smoking, a sensation in his head similar to that when riding on a carousel, incongruous thoughts whirling round dizzily, his mind not registering things rationally. She had gasped for breath as if drowning – or suffocating – and they had interpreted his panic as an act, theatrical. That was why they were going to call the Police. They would arrest him on suspicion of murder. But he was innocent. She had died of natural causes. And the three children needed him more than ever. They were leaving Lima within three months, the five of them. It was a mistake. She couldn't be dead, not really. If she were it was his fault for failing to get a doctor when she'd first awoken. If he had acted sooner the Clinic could have saved her.

Two detectives arrived. One of them recognised Rick immediately having seen him at the *Comisaría* a few weeks before. He smiled, but coolly and asked him what had happened. Briefly, Rick told him.

'*Bien*,' he said. 'There's nothing we can do here at the moment. I'll have to accompany you to your apartment. Is that OK? Have you got transport?'

'Yes,' Rick said.

'Good, I'll follow you then. Which car is it?'

'The white VW just outside.'

'Señora Vargas was still weeping, but Rick was dry-eyed. As they drove back he kept an eye on the mirror, watching the police-car behind them. He would have to get up to the flat first. They turned into the entrance and while Señora Vargas was parking Rick got out and ran to the lift. It closed as the police-car was drawing up outside the building. Rick went up to the seventh floor, let himself into his flat, opened the drawer of his desk, took out the bundle of marijuana Alberto had given him and which was wrapped in brown paper, nipped outside and threw it down the rubbish chute. At that moment the detective emerged from the lift.

Inside the flat he had a cursory look round the cabinets in the bathroom and cupboards in the kitchen. He examined Jean's dressing-table thoroughly and glanced at Rick's desk, opening the top drawer, but not the bottom one where the marijuana had been.

'Are you sure there are no tranquilisers or sleeping-tablets in the place?' he said.

'No, nothing.'

'No cocaine or marijuana?'

'No, you can search everywhere. My wife never touched stuff like that anyway.'

'All right,' he said smiling. 'I'm sorry about these questions at a time like this, but they are necessary. Tell me – was your wife taking the contraceptive pill?'

'Yes.'

'For how long, do you know?'

'Since my son was born. About three years.'

'Can you find them for me?'

'I think so.'

Rick found the pills in a handbag. came back and gave them to the detective. He jotted something down in his notebook and kept the pills.

'*Muy bien*,' he said. 'I'll give you time to make arrangements for the children, then I want to see you back at the American Clinic. In about an hour. There are a lot of details to straighten out. Of course, there will have to be an autopsy. Then there's the funeral. It has to take place within forty-eight hours. That's the law here.'

When the detective had left Rick used the Italians' flat to phone Doctor Delgado, Alberto and Cathy, then Irma. Irma said that she would come round and take the children out for the day. The others arranged to meet him at the Clinic. Within a few minutes Irma arrived. Instinctively Rick embraced her, holding her tight.

'Thank you for coming,' he said.

'Richard, I can't believe it,' she said. 'I'm so sorry.'

'It was so quick,' he managed to say.

'Don't talk now,' she said. 'I'll take the children and you can go back to the hospital and do what has to be done.'

The children were dressed and ready. The Indian maid, Isolina, herself red-eyed and still in tears, had seen to that.

'Where's mummy?' Sara asked.

'She's very sick,' Rick said. 'We had to take her to hospital.'

'Poor mummy.'

He had to get out of the flat. He kissed the children and left them with Irma, unable to look directly at any of them.

At the Clinic the detective was waiting. 'They say your wife died of a haemorrhage of the lung,' he said. 'Of course, there will still have to be a post-mortem so the body will be transferred to the Lima morgue. I shall have to ask you to report to the *Comisaría* later this afternoon – to make a proper statement. If you want to see your wife she is in the chapel now.'

In the chapel Jean, covered by a sheet, was laid out on a slab beneath a crucifix. Her jaw was still dropped, her mouth open, her face quite lined and her once gold-coloured hair faded and coarse. The look of surprise which he remembered from the dawn had ossified upon her face. She looked older than her age. He drew back the sheet a fraction further. There were dark mottled patches over her upper chest and shoulders. He covered her again, put his lips to her cheek for a moment, then walked abruptly away.

In the waiting-room he met Alberto, Cathy and Doctor Delgado. Their faces were drawn, puzzled rather than shocked. Alberto put his arms round Rick's shoulders.

'Jesus, man!' he said. 'What can I say?'

Cathy embraced him and Delgado put his hand protectively upon Rick's arm. Then at Cath's suggestion they went into the restaurant where Alberto ordered coffee.

'I just can't believe it,' Cathy said. 'She seemed fine last night at dinner.'

'What happened?' Alberto said.

'Don't talk about it if you don't want to,' Cath said. But once again Rick explained the circumstances. It was the third time, but oddly it seemed to help. The bare narrative was beginning to give her death some semblance of reality.

'Richard,' Delgado said. 'I'm going to release you from your contract right away. There's only another month and we'll manage. You'll have a lot to arrange. It's going to be a busy week or two for you.'

'Have you thought about what you're going to do now?' Cathy said. Until that moment he hadn't.

'As soon as I've got everything settled her,' he said, 'I'll take the children back to England. We were leaving at the end of the year anyway.'

'Only time will help,' Delgado said. 'It must be a terrible shock, but time is the great healer.'

Rick lit another cigarette. His hand trembled a little and his mouth was dry. He could feel another spasm of diarrhoea coming on. He tightened his sphincter muscles and shifted on his seat.

'Could you help me to arrange things?' he said to Alberto.

'We'll do anything we can to help,' Cathy said.

Cathy and Delgado had to leave. On her way home Cath didn't know precisely what she was feeling except a sense of being profoundly disturbed. Jean had always seemed much fitter than Cath herself. She would have to get out of this country as soon as possible. It was absolutely pointless carrying on with a screwed-up marriage. Life was too tenuous, too short. There simply wasn't time to mess around. Surely Alberto would see that now. When someone as close to you as

Jean died it brought you down to essentials with a crash. And that meant leaving Peru, getting the children to the States, finding a job there, obtaining a divorce. There was no going back. And no point in wasting time.

Alberto and Rick saw the Registrar at the Clinic to arrange for removal of the body. Alberto did most of the talking. He arranged for the funeral to take place at the Lima cemetery, El Angel. It was to be the following afternoon, a Sunday, and All Saints Day. Once these arrangements were finalised they drove down to the seafront at Miraflores. They went to a cafe on the cliffs overlooking the bay with its lines of white breakers rolling in. Alberto ordered steak and wine, but Rick didn't feel like eating. He chewed on the meat, then pushed the plate aside and drank the wine.

Afterwards they sat drinking whiskey for an hour, but it did nothing to erase Rick's memories of the morning. Later they drove down to the beach at Agua Dulce, sat on the sand and watched the fresh-water streams that cascaded down the cliff face. Emerald foliage clung to the rock and beyond were skeins of purple, scarlet and orange bougainvillaea. It was a warm day, the first real heat of summer and the beach was crowded with boys playing football and dark-skinned girls sunbathing. Everyone seemed to be smiling in the sun. Rick scuffed the sand with his leather shoes, his dry eyes itchy, a burning sensation behind them as if they were full of chlorine. At four o'clock Alberto drove him to the *Comisaria* where he had to report to the detective, then they went to the main Post Office. From there he sent a telegram to his brother in England. After that Alberto dropped him at his apartment.

'I'll come round later, man,' he said. 'Try to get some sleep, it'll do you good.'

Once on his own he lay face down on the bed. He felt drained, but still could not believe in the reality of events, not quite. Last night he and Jean had actually made love. That was scarcely fifteen hours ago, but it seemed like an incident from the remote past. At teatime Irma brought the children back. They were laughing, excited by their day out.

'The funeral's tomorrow,' he said to Irma.

'I shan't come myself,' she said. 'But I'd like to help you as much as I can so I'll have the children again tomorrow. You won't be taking them with you, will you?'

'No, I don't think so,' he said. 'I don't feel like facing it myself.'

'But you must,' Irma said. 'And if you want to borrow my car for any reason, you can, you know that.'

'What's happened to mummy?' asked Sara who had come into the room.

'Listen,' Rick said. 'I've got to tell you something.'

'I think I'll go now,' Irma said. 'I'll call round early tomorrow and the kids can come to my place.'

'Mummy was very sick last night,' Rick said after Irma had left. 'And the doctors couldn't do anything to help her at the hospital.'

'Did she die?' Sara said. Rick nodded. At that moment he began to weep. Sara put her arms round him, trying to comfort him. David didn't really understand at all. He looked mystified. Rick held his daughters to him for a moment, then poured himself a shot of *pisco*, drinking it in one gulp.

That night Alberto and Cath took him out to a Chinese restaurant for dinner. He could eat little but drank continuously. His nose was streaming as if he had a cold and his mouth was dry. In bed later he couldn't sleep despite the alcohol. Fear made him sit up and light a cigarette while the events of the morning continued to run through his mind, obsessively. In the early hours Sara climbed into bed with him. He hugged her small five-year old body and finally slept. Waking on Sunday morning was like returning to a bad dream from which sleep had given him some respite. He dressed the children and got them ready for Irma, and drank several cups of black coffee. His doctor called by and gave him some tranquilisers for the afternoon. Soon afterwards Alberto arrived and they went to the *Comisaria* for Rick to report. The police still didn't take a detailed statement. They were waiting for the post-mortem. A detective accompanied them to the Lima morgue and was given the result of the autopsy.

'It says your wife died of a pulmonary endaema,' the detective said.

'What does that mean?'

'It's the medical term for a haemorrhage of the lung,' Alberto said.

'But what was the cause?'

'It doesn't say,' the detective said. 'There was no single cause but so far as we're concerned the funeral can go ahead as arranged. It seems you're in the clear. We'd just like your statement first thing tomorrow morning.'

'I'd like to know what actually caused it,' Rick said.

'They don't know,' Alberto said. 'It could have been a virus or an asthmatic attack, anything. But there's nothing you could have done, Rick, so don't feel guilty. Do you want to see the body?'

'Yes.'

'Well, let me go first.' A few minutes later Alberto was back. 'Look, Rick,' he said. 'If I were you I'd leave it.'

'Why?'

'The body's been cut open, it's not a pleasant sight, believe me. It won't do you any good to see it.'

The funeral was at three o'clock. Rick went to Irma's to have some lunch with the children, then met Alberto again at the mortician's. Many of his friends and acquaintances were already there, but he was so heavily tranquilised that events seemed to be happening at several removes. He felt distant, remote, though his senses, probably because of the drug, were alert, stimulated. The coffin was on a table behind some curtains and people were filing past to pay their last respects. Rick looked at it once, briefly. It was covered in roses and carnations, dark red against the black. A small window was cut in the coffin's lid and through it Jean's face was thin and pale, the beginning of a cut just visible above the black dress they had put her in. There was a faint smell in the place, a peculiar combination of incense, disinfectant and, in his imagination, decay. Seeing Jean there he felt a rush of anger. She looked so vulnerable stretched out in that black coffin for people to stare at. But nothing mattered to her anymore; the body was a husk, a shell on the sea-shore. She was nothing; the dead were nothing. She was beyond everything now, invulnerable, he thought, as they drove to the cemetery in the shadow of the grey foothills.

Because this was All Saints Day, the streets of La Victoria were jammed with cars. In one section the procession was held up and Alberto got separated from the other cars. On either side of the road were lines of stalls selling pastries, sweet-meats and grilled meat on skewers. The bars were full of drunks who came reeling out to join the throng. Most were Indians carrying flowers and wending their way to the cemetery. All Saints Day – the Catholic celebration of death and the after-life! Jean would surely have appreciated the irony herself.

Alberto was finally forced to park the car a few blocks from the cemetery and they walked the rest of the way. An aroma of spices and flowers, burning charcoal and incense filled the air. Although strangely detached, Rick's senses were sharp as if he had been smoking marijuana. What drug had the doctor given him? Young honey-coloured women with sensuous bodies flirted with the passers-by and gave the streets a festive, almost an erotic atmosphere. Rick felt a little guilty that even on such an occasion he was aware of this. No matter how emotionally numb he might feel, his senses responded.

They were sweating when they joined the other mourners just inside the cemetery gates. The coffin was resting on a small altar around which his friends had formed a half-circle. A priest came up to them and although Rick waved him away he genuflected and said a few perfunctory words above the coffin. A Catholic funeral and Jean was, at the very least, an agnostic. She would have preferred cremation, Rick knew as she'd once mentioned this, but it was illegal in Catholic Peru.

Some of Rick's colleagues from the college hitched the coffin onto their shoulders and began to move off, the rest following behind. The bearers staggered along in the heat, sweating in their dark suits, between concrete blocks like rectangular beehives. The ground was bare and brown, devoid of grass, with builders' rubble scattered about in piles on the baked-mud surface. They continued for a mile through this almost labyrinthine complex until arriving at the site. Jean's niche was numbered A-28. There the stonemason, an Indian, inserted the coffin into the arched-black compartment. Rick stood back with the others watching him fit the concrete slab into place and seal it up with fresh cement. It took about twenty minutes. Rick could taste bile in his mouth. He smoked a cigarette and looked at Cathy. She had a hand poised tentatively in front of her mouth. At last the stone-mason carved the name, JEAN PRESTON, in capitals on the wet cement. It was over.

'Let's go,' Rick said to Alberto. He thanked the others for coming and they all shook hands with him, then followed by Alberto and Cath, Rick hurried through the ornate gates and along the still crowded streets to the car.

The following week passed quickly enough and left Rick little time for either self-pity or grief. It was enough to get through each moment, each day as it came. He reported to the *Comisaria*, made his official statement and was cleared by the police. He went through the bureaucratic machinery at the Ministries of Taxation and Justice to obtain tax-clearance and permission to leave the country with his three children. He cancelled their passage on the Italian ship and booked a flight with BOAC to London. He paid off his debts, arranged for Alberto to sell his furniture to cover outstanding rent, packed his personal possessions and sent them by sea. He gave most of Jean's clothes to the maid, Isolina, who stayed on at the flat to help him. He went to the college, collected his salary and changed it into sterling. All this took ten days of frantic activity. He ate little, smoked too much, and lost a stone in weight.

Alberto and Cathy helped him through by calling round as frequently as they were able, but the most difficult time was when he found himself alone late at night. He should have been far more attentive to Jean; should have been more sympathetic and affectionate; should have treated her better. It was only when someone you loved died, he reflected, that you appreciated that person properly.

He looked through their recent photographs, trying to determine whether Jean had any premonition or knowledge of her illness. In one snapshot he had caught her looking towards the foothills above the river at their favourite picnic-spot, emerald ferns behind her and white pebbles in the foreground. Wearing her red jumper and black skirt, she looked slimmer than he could recall and rather pallid. He even thought he could detect a wistful expression upon her face. Once he woke up in a cold sweat, having dreamed that in some obscure way he had actually been responsible for her death and the police were aware of this but unable to prove anything. Perhaps his insensitivity and blindness had in a very real sense destroyed her, he thought.

At times he woke up at night too scared to sleep, fear adding a further impurity to his grief. Having witnessed sudden death he was only too conscious of the fragility of anyone's hold on life. And for the first time in years he was completely on his own apart from the children. Jean had gone and it was as if part of him had been amputated. He now had sole responsibility for the kids and sometimes when he looked at them he almost cracked up with the weight of it. His daughter, Sara, had been born in Lima and now the place had exacted its price. It had taken Jean. She had paid for their exile, voluntary though that had been, and Rick had been cheated by a malevolent trick of fate. Such notions almost unbalanced him. He felt as if we were on the edge of a precipice and within an ace of falling over it. Sometimes he felt that the children had been irreparably deprived, their lives permanently damaged, and then he wanted to shout abuse at some power outside himself – at God in whom he had never believed.

One afternoon a few days before leaving Peru he was driving Irma's blue sports-car out to the fishing port, Chorrillos, at the far end of the bay. It was almost summer and very warm. Dark-haired and plump, Irma was sitting beside him and their children were cramped into the space behind the front-seat. Rick put his foot down and the powerful little car shot forward and accelerated along the winding road between the brown cliffs and grey ocean. It was close to sunset. In the distance the skyscrapers of Lima were blurred in thin mist and the fishing-boats moored at the jetty beneath them motionless against the dull reddish glow of the sun. And quite unexpectedly Rick felt a momentary elation.

For the first time since it had happened he felt that he could accept the fact of Jean's death. The dead were nothing, *nada*, while he himself had a life ahead though he'd no idea what course it would take. It was an unknown quantity, but he was only in his mid-thirties, a young man still. And his future, which had been intertwined with Jean's, was now a blank, unmapped and uncharted. For a moment this idea exhilarated him. Tentatively, he formulated the thought again. It was still there like a gleam of hope: he was alive and free.

'Why don't you come round later tonight?' he said. 'Let's go out to dinner and afterwards we can have a drink.'

'I'd like that,' Irma said. Sitting beside her in the car, his thigh pressed against hers, Rick felt the warmth of desire for the first time since that Saturday two weeks before.

That night after Isolina had cooked their supper, Rick bathed the children and tucked them up in bed. He had a shower himself, then dressed carefully in his favourite shirt and maroon-suede jacket. He mixed himself a drink, put on a Dylan album and waited for Irma. She was late and he had drunk two whiskies by the time she called. He let her in, kissed her, and suddenly she held him tight, clinging to him, and shaken by sobs. He kissed her wet face, her eyelids, her neck, her mouth.

'Rick, Rick,' she said. 'I've felt so confused the last couple of weeks, thinking about Jean and you and everything that's happened . . .'

'I want you.'

'I don't know what I feel anymore, it's all been so unreal and disturbing.'

'Let's make love.'

'I thought I only wanted you as a friend and now this has happened to Jean – oh I don't know, I don't know anything anymore.'

'Don't talk about it.'

'Let's go out,' she said. 'Is it all right to leave the kids?'

'Yes, Isolina is going to babysit.'

Rick drove her sports-car to an Argentine restaurant in Magdalena. There they had steaks and two bottles of Chilean wine while a group of musicians played the melancholy folk-songs of the pampas. The place itself was crowded, full of people enjoying themselves noisily. Afterwards Rick suggested going back to his apartment.

'No,' she said. 'It would feel strange there. It wouldn't be right somehow. I'd prefer the anonymity of that motel.'

He drove up the central highway to *Tu y Yo*. Once in the hired room with the mirrors they undressed quickly and clung to each other, laughing from the release of what seemed unbearable tension. They made love twice in the hour, the second time Irma astride him, her hair tickling his mouth. It was the first time Rick had laughed in the

163

last two weeks. He felt as if he were taking strength from her body so that he was able to banish that lingering fear which had been with him continuously. In a peculiar way Jean's death had intensified their lovemaking. It was a re-affirmation of life, something Rick felt he needed almost more than he'd ever done previously. He wondered whether Jean would have reacted similarly had she been the one left and imagined she would. Once, while they were actually making love, an image of Jean's face – the dropped jaw and transformed eyes, – came into his mind, but it no longer haunted him.

Because Rick was leaving in a few days there seemed to be no barriers between them and no time to be cautious or defensive. They were only able to visit the motel on one more occasion, the morning before Rick was flying home, an hour together, a fleeting interlude that for Rick seemed like a talisman against bad luck.

That same afternoon Alberto and Cath took him to the beach at Punta Hermosa. Rick went in for a last swim there, plunging through the breakers and out towards the point. Mackerel were jumping and three dolphins entered the bay to corral the fish, but he felt no fear, only a bitter-sweet joy at being alive. When he thought of Jean it was not with bitterness, but genuine sorrow because she had been deprived of this joy.

After he had dried himself and dressed, they walked along the sandy headland above the cliffs, the children running in front, Alberto entertaining them, Cathy strolling with Rick.

'It's strange,' she said, 'and I don't know whether I should tell you this, whether you would understand or not, but . . .'

'Don't tell me you and Alberto are getting back together again.'

'No, not exactly, but we're at least friends again and that seems to me important.'

'Well, I'm glad about that,' he said. 'I'm fond of you both and always have been.'

'When I look back on our rows,' she said, 'they seem so silly and trivial, but I still want to go back to the States and take the kids. I think we'll probably end up getting divorced.'

'You really want that?'

'We're very different, Alberto and I, and living together has been so destructive for us both. We'll be better off on our own and I think we can work things out in a friendly manner.'

'I hope so,' Rick said, thinking that the solution to his marital problems had been simple and drastic. Relationships had had a tendency to resolve themselves during the last few weeks, he thought, some of his bitterness returning.

'What I really wanted to say though was this – and I just hope it won't upset you,' Cath continued, 'but the whole absurd business, Jean dying just like that I mean, made me see what is important. Put things in perspective, if you can understand that.'

'I think I can,' he said.

'It's ironic that it should take such a terrible tragedy to make you see your own life more clearly,' she said, 'but I suppose that's always the way. And I can't deny it.'

'You don't have to explain or feel guilty about it,' Rick said.

'I don't,' she said. 'When you phoned me that morning I was so angry – that a person such as Jean – and we loved her, you must know that – should die in such a way. But something has come out of that sadness. You don't mind me telling you all this, do you?'

'Of course not.'

'It shocked everyone,' Cath said. 'And I still feel angry about it – so God knows what you must be going through. But I want you to know how much we feel for you and the kids. You must write and keep in touch. We're going to miss you, I mean it.'

Irma drove Rick to the airport the following morning while Cath and Alberto took his three children. In the lounge they were joined by Doctor Delgado and his wife who gave each of the children a woollen llama, clapped Rick on the shoulders and wished him *luck*. Cath frowned at the inappropriate choice of phrase. It was part of their strained attempt, she supposed, to make the departure seem normal. In fact the tension was positively tangible. She could see that Rick was anxious to board the plane, to be gone, and the others seemed just as eager at this stage to see him go. Watching Rick, his face thinner and tight, she wondered how much bitterness he really felt towards Lima. At the same time, despite all that had happened to him, she was faintly envious. His grief would slowly fade and he would soon be alone in a different country. Of course, he would have to learn how to cope with three children just as she and every mother had learned, but he was about to make a new start.

When his flight was announced Cath kissed him at the barrier, then stood aside while Irma did the same. She wondered whether they had been having an affair and if so whether it had started before or after Jean's death. Either way, it was natural, she supposed. It was life asserting itself no matter what the moralists might think.

Then pushing his hand-luggage and David in a trolley, Emma and Sara tagging behind him, Rick turned away and was soon lost among the other passengers, but that last image stayed in Cath's mind for some minutes. He had looked for a moment so vulnerable and isolated, but then he was resilient enough. It was the children she really felt sorry for. They were the ones who suffered the worst at such times. And they did so without self-pity or complaint.

'Do you want to go up and watch the take-off?' Alberto said.

'Not really,' she said. 'There's not much point. I'd prefer to get home. I promised to take the kids to the beach.'

On the drive back she was silent, thinking that now they had all gone – Robert and Sheila, Julio and Rick. And Jean was dead. Only she and Alberto remained. And sad though this made her, she was determined that next time she came to the airport it would be because she herself was leaving.

ACKNOWLEDGEMENTS

Chapter 3 was first published under the title, *Revolution* in *Ambit* 110; Chapter 4 was published under the title, *Green Witch*, in the Arts Council anthology, *New Stories 2*; a section of Chapter 6 was published in *Iron*; Chapter 7 was published in *Not Poetry* under the title, *Earthquake*; short sections of Chapter 6 and 9 were published in *Argo* and an earlier version of the opening section of Chapter 9 was published under the title *Arrest* in *Ambit* 99.